The Hopeful Duke

By

Leah Toole

The Hopeful Duke

Copyright © 2025 Leah Toole. All rights reserved.

All rights reserved. No part of this publication may be reproduced, stored, or transmitted in any form or by any means, whether electronic, mechanical, or photocopying, recording, scanning, or otherwise without written permission from the author.
It is illegal to copy this book, post it to a website, or distribute it by any other means without permission.

Also by Leah Toole

The Tudor Heirs Series

I – The Saddest Princess

...

II – The Haunted Queen

...

III – The Puppet King

...

IV – The Forgotten Prince

~

The Rose and the Pomegranate

~

1500

Praise for the Novels of The Tudor Heirs Series:

"Tender and vivid descriptions expanding our usual picture of this segment of Henry and Katherine. I recommend these books to any and all fans of the period from Henry VIII through to his sixth wife Catherine Parr and throughout the reign of Elizabeth I."

- USA

"Couldn't put this one down! Oh, and that surprise towards the end though! Absolutely loved this book! Another great book from Leah!"

- USA

"Absolutely adored 'The Saddest Princess' about Mary I. It was so well-written, and such a gripping read. I read it all in one go, and it's the best book I've ever read. Many thanks to the author for writing this masterpiece!"

- UK

"Very Interesting Perspective.
I have thoroughly enjoyed reading the Tudor Heir series. I think this book [The Puppet King] has the most interesting perspective of the life of Edward VI.
I never knew much about Edward VI's reign but even though this book is fiction I feel like I have learnt quite a bit about the key points in history.
If you are into the Tudor era I highly recommend this series."

- UK

To my readers, who mass requested
a book about Henry Fitzroy.
I hope I was able to deliver with this
addition to the Tudor Heirs Series.

Prologue:

19th May 1536
Tower of London, Tower Green

I watch from among the crowd of over a thousand people as Anne Boleyn speaks her last, then kneels before the French swordsman.

Her words were eloquent, calm. But I can see now that her hands are shaking before her as she is blindfolded from behind. A smile twitches at the corners of my mouth, and I clear my throat to hide my elation.

Then the sword takes her head clean off.

You ought to thank God for having escaped from the hands of that woman, who had planned your death by poison.

The king's words spoken to me on the day of Anne Boleyn's arrest echo in my mind, and I breathe a slow sigh of relief to see that I am finally safe now that she is dead.

A low moan of disgust escapes the people around me when her head *thumps* audibly on the wooden scaffold, some cringing, some staring wide-eyed in fascination.

But I do not react, for I have no other feeling but alleviation.

I am here on behalf of my king, to represent him – my presence at his wife's beheading indicating to the world that the king approved of what was happening.

It is not the first time I have attended an execution in the name of Henry VIII. As a member of the royal family, it is one of the many duties bestowed onto me by my king. And I have gladly accepted them all throughout the years; I am honoured to, in fact. Anything to respect my father's wishes and prove myself worthy.

I was born a bastard, you see.

One of many, I am sure…

But I was the only one the king chose to claim as his own when he named me after himself: Henry.

It was my surname that set me apart from all the others, however, for I was not named after my mother – Blount – nor after the man who she would go on to marry after my birth.

No, my surname is Fitzroy. Which, as I learned in my childhood, quite literally translates into *Son of the King*.

I am King Henry VIII's own bastard son. The very son that proved to the monarch that he could, in fact, sire healthy male children.

My birth – I have been told – was widely celebrated despite my illegitimate status, and the king gleefully showed me off to the court and country as proof of his virility and strength.

And yet…as the years went on, the novelty of my existence wore off for my father, and he became distracted by other things.

Or, more precisely, by the woman who he believed would bear him a *real* son. One of legitimate birth.

Now, I force myself to look right at that very woman as she lay dead before me, crimson blood spurting from her severed neck as her ladies-in-waiting sob into handkerchiefs all around her.

Did I think this would happen?

Of course not. No one did. Not even her greatest enemies, those who had hated her from the beginning, could have predicted this outcome – the first in English history – for no Queen Consort had ever been dispatched by beheading at the order of the king.

I hear her ladies panicking then, once they realise that Henry VIII had failed to arrange for a coffin to be prepared for his former wife. Three of them scuttle off, clunking heavily down the wooden steps in search of whatever chest may be suitable to fit Anne Boleyn's body.

And then I turn to leave, my role having been fulfilled the moment her heart had stopped beating. I make my way through the throng of astonished onlookers. Some of them are crying, some grinning, some craning their necks in awe to catch a better glimpse of the horrific scene. But, as I expected, most are stunned into silence; astounded to witness how one who the king had risen so high could be cut down so cruelly.

Chapter 1

January 1514
Greenwich Palace, London

Elizabeth Blount was nothing short of ecstatic to have been selected to dance with the King of England during the New Year's masque.
At just twelve years old, the young girl had entered Queen Katherine of Aragon's household a few months earlier and had since then become known throughout the English court as 'the beauty among the queen's entourage'.
She had quickly received some attention from several of the male courtiers, one of which was the king's closest friend, Charles Brandon, who, at thirty-years-old, made Elizabeth feel a little uneasy. But her father had assured her it was no more than harmless flirtation, and even encouraged her to play into the older man's affections.
A marriage to the king's dearest friend – and a duke! – cannot be a bad match.
Elizabeth – who everyone called Bessie – had not known exactly *how* to engage in flirtation with the duke, and she had often found herself flushing with embarrassment whenever she locked eyes with him. She did not want his attention, no matter what her father said.
But over the months that followed, whatever she did – or did not do – must not have worked in her favour, for Charles Brandon appeared to have suddenly lost interest, and Bessie relaxed to think she was free of adult affairs once again.
Now, as she awaited her cue to emerge from among the crowd to join in the masque, Bessie could not help but bounce her leg excitedly underneath her dress of blue velvet. It was a stunning piece, cut in the fashion of Savoy and completed with a silver cloak and a bonnet of burned gold. It was, quite frankly, the most exquisite ensemble the young girl had ever worn.

Born to John Blount and Katherine Peshall Blount, Bessie was educated to possess all the much-desired attributes for a queen's lady-in-waiting. Grace and good manners had come easily to Bessie, who – as her mother had often told her – was good-natured at heart. But it was the more fun requirements that Bessie not only enjoyed the most, but also strived to master. Dancing and singing were Bessie's passions, as well as playing the lute, which – to the court's amusement – she did exceptionally well. And it was precisely these skills that had led to her being chosen to partner with the king during this special masquerade to celebrate the New Year.

It was time, the chiming of the bells signalling Bessie's call to action, and she rose from among the queen's ladies like the Greek goddess Gaia, springing to life from the Earth.

The crowd gasped and clapped in admiration of her as she strode elegantly towards the king at the centre of the performance, the velvet rustling luxuriously as she moved.

"My Lady," the king said as he bowed at the waist and extended his hand.

He was wearing a mask and was disguised in clothing equal to that of his fellow dancers, but it was clear to the whole court that this was their young and handsome King Henry VIII, for he stood tallest among the others, and his orange hair burned as bright as a flame.

Bessie took his outstretched hand, hers feeling suddenly very small, and took a step towards him, grinning widely to know that she was the luckiest girl in all of England to share this special dance with him.

Henry VIII had been crowned King of England five years prior upon the death of his father, Henry Tudor.

Henry Tudor had not been a well-liked king, having obtained the throne of England in combat against the Yorkist King Richard III. He had won the crown on the battlefield as a usurper – a jibe which would remain associated with him throughout his reign. He had been accepted by the people, however, when he swiftly married the much-loved Elizabeth of York: the princess niece of Richard III, and the white rose of York to his red rose of Lancaster. Their union had ended the thirty-year long civil war, the War of the Roses, and for that at least, the English people had tolerated Henry Tudor as their king.

His decades-long reign had settled into a relatively calm one following the first few years of uncertainty, but with the sudden death of their beloved teenaged son Prince Arthur in 1502, as well as Queen Elizabeth of York's death just a year thereafter, Henry Tudor had become unfavourable yet again. Not only for the lack of their beloved queen, but also for the vast contrast between him – a now old, tight-fisted, money loving king who passed dastardly taxations to control the nobles and the people – and his only surviving heir, Prince Harry, who had grown up to become a vivacious, athletic, and charismatic young man.

Over the years that followed, the people had made their preference of their prince over their king very clear, so much so that in 1508 Henry Tudor had felt the need to lock up his remaining son under the pretence that 'he must be kept safe from harm as his only surviving heir.'

It was not an untruth, for his only son's survival was imperative for the continuation of the Tudor dynasty.

But, beyond that, Henry Tudor had become paranoid of his son's palpable popularity. And he had begun to fear an uprising, a usurpation just as he himself had done to Richard III.

At the time, Prince Harry, too, had felt the shift within the court and council, as though they cared more for *his* opinions than that of their monarch. But there had not been a bone in the prince's body which had planned, or even considered, usurping his father, for Prince Harry cared little for the tediousness of running the country, favouring the more entertaining aspects of life.

Henry Tudor need not have worried so much – and he may have lived longer had he not – for just a year later in 1509, King Henry Tudor was pronounced dead of consumption, and his second-born son was proclaimed king through right of inheritance, not overthrowal.

And the young King Henry VIII only wished never to feel trapped again, or indeed, to ever allow for his father's paranoia to take the heart of him.

April 1514

Since his joint coronation with his beloved wife, Katherine of Aragon, the young king had experienced his fair share of disappointments, both within his marriage and in his reign.
As the second-born son to his royal mother and father, King Henry VIII was not supposed to have ascended the throne, his entire childhood having been focused on pursuing priesthood. His older brother, Arthur, had been destined to become king, but he had tragically died at the age of fifteen, leading his younger brother to fill his shoes. And they had been big shoes to fill.
Because of this turn of events, King Henry was more aware than anyone that for a monarch to have a safe and stable reign, he must make sure to sire *at least* two sons by his legal wife – one to succeed him, the other as a failsafe, just as he himself had been.
But disastrously, the king and queen had not had much luck when it came to creating a family, Katherine of Aragon having suffered one miscarriage and a stillbirth since their wedding five years prior, as well as the devastatingly premature death of their infant son, Henry Duke of Cornwall in 1511.
Baby Hal's death had hit them hard, Henry and Katherine only having managed to move past it through their genuine love for one another. Henry had been exceptionally comforting in the months that had followed their baby's loss, the whole court noting that their queen very likely only survived the heartbreak because of the king's affections.
But, as yet unbeknownst to the court, his patience was wearing thin of late, because there was only for so long that a man could comfort his wife before he had to consider that perhaps she was somehow the problem…

After all, the production of children was a woman's domain, and if after half a decade of marriage the king had nothing to show for his efforts…who else but his wife could be responsible?
Nevertheless, Henry adored Katherine.
She was the epitome of queenship. The moon to his stars. The cream to his pie. The Aphrodite to his Adonis –

"There is talk that King Ferdinand, the queen's own father, will renege the treaty to attack France," King Henry's advisor, Thomas Wolsey, now told him, interrupting his thoughts and briefly catapulting his appreciation for his wife into resentment.

"The new Pope, Leo X, is encouraging peace…" Wolsey concluded.

"Peace," Henry echoed, chewing on the word as though to identify its flavour. Then his top lip involuntarily curled up in disgust.

"This is treachery!" the young king bellowed, causing several courtiers to look his way as he and Wolsey attempted to discuss the matter in the great hall.
Wolsey looked over his shoulder, then back to his king as he stood furiously before him.

"What of our troops?" Henry demanded, "This campaign cannot fail, Wolsey!"
The man of the cloth inhaled slowly, suggesting to the younger man not only that he was pondering his response, but also that the king ought to exercise some patience.
But picking up on subtleties was not one of the young king's fortes.

"It is but rumours for now, Your Highness," Wolsey reminded Henry, "But if your father-in-law does indeed fail to stick to the terms of our treaty to invade France together, then I see no other option but to settle for peace with France after all."

"Peace?!" the king exclaimed, "With England's sworn enemy?"
He shook his head while Wolsey nodded his.

"It would be a pity…" the older man mumbled after a moment.
Henry looked up, "What?"

Wolsey cocked his head to one side, screwed up his face as if he were deliberating his choice of words, though he had already practiced them extensively before even meeting with the king that morning.

"It would be a pity if our alliance with Spain were to prove useless in this pursuit."

Henry looked over Wolsey's shoulder then as Katherine and her ladies-in-waiting entered the great hall, the Spanish queen laughing gently at a remark from one of her entourage.

Katherine must have sensed his gaze on her, for she met it from across the vast room and smiled lovingly at him.

"Yes," Henry said then, failing to return his wife's warmth, "It would be a pity, indeed."

Since Katherine's most recent loss back in September of the previous year, she and Henry had been trying – and failing – to conceive again.

Their amorous rendezvous were a regular occurrence, the young king making sure to share a bed with his wife at least three times a week. Because even above expansion and military success, the production of an heir was paramount.

Now, as he thrusted mechanically over her on their fourth coupling that week, Henry pondered back to the time when he had been eager – nay, *aching* – to make love to his wife. Back when their union had been one of much desire and excitement. When they had not yet been plagued by the memories of their grief, and the early days of his reign and marriage had promised nothing but triumph.

That is not to say that Henry was no longer in love with his wife. He was! He cherished her above all others, cared for her wellbeing and respected her opinions. His first thoughts in the morning were always of her.

But, over the years, their sexual encounters had gone from passionate and explorational to transactional. Their once ardent relationship having been chiselled down from a sturdy slab of wood to a delicate trinket. One that might break at the slightest touch.

Henry knew when it had *really* begun, however. And he could not rightly blame all their marital cracks on Katherine's failed pregnancies, for Henry himself had played a part in pushing Katherine away.

The first mistress he ever took was Anne, the Lady Hastings, back in 1510.

Katherine had been with child for the second time then, and the king's physicians had recommended he take a mistress to relieve himself while the queen could not fulfil her marital duties in the bedroom.

He had been opposed to the idea for a long while, not really having *wanted* another woman at the time. His father, Henry Tudor, had never taken a mistress during his marriage to Elizabeth of York. And Henry had planned to lead by his father's example – in that, at least.

But the ache to engage in intimacy had been too strong, and the risk to do so with his pregnant wife too great.

There had been no other way.

He had felt guilty for a time, had tried to keep his affair hidden even, by persuading his good friend William Compton to take the fall when Anne Hastings' husband had found out of her adultery and sent her to a nunnery.

But Katherine had seen through the charade, had known Anne Hastings' true lover to have been the king, and not Compton, no matter how much he claimed otherwise.

It had led to their first clash of words, and the first fracture in their once perfect marriage.

Since then, Henry had entertained one other, a former tutor of his sisters' named Jane Popincourt. She had, with her French wiles, opened the king's eyes to a more adventurous lovemaking. One that, while incredibly satisfying, he would not *dare* to disrespect his wife with! Jane Popincourt had blown the young king's mind in more ways than one, to say the least, and while Henry would never wish for his wife to behave in such a manner in the bedroom – for it was, quite frankly, lewd – laying with Katherine now felt lacklustre in comparison.

And so, Katherine's quiet resentment of him – paired with his newfound knowledge of more depraved things – made for a cold meeting of bodies and minds…and Henry would often have to think of Jane Popincourt to be able to climax when laying with his wife.

It was what he had to do now, for his arm muscles had begun to cramp with the extended time hovering over Katherine. And with a shameful shudder, Henry exhaled with relief.

The queen smiled tightly up at him when he had finally finished, only just falling short of thanking him before he rolled off of her.

"Would you care to stay the night, my lord?" Katherine asked gently as they both lay on their backs, looking up at the wood carved panel of the four-poster bed. Her Spanish accent was still strong despite living in England for fifteen years.

It was something Henry had found attractive once. And a lump of guilt formed in his throat to think he only found it tedious of late.

Feeling ashamed of his need to think of another during his private time with his beloved, the king responded by taking Katherine in his arms and laying her head on his toned chest.

Katherine smiled to herself before closing her eyes, her husband's heart beating loudly in her ear as he gently stroked her long hair.

In the blurry edges of sleep, dark thoughts threatened to invade Katherine's calm then, memories of her grief attempting to sully the tender moment with her husband. Her lost children never being far from her mind.

She sighed deeply and nestled closer to Henry, forcing herself to shut out her misery, and to focus instead on the potential child they may well have conceived that very moment.

And though married before God and physically closer than they could possibly be, the king and queen drifted off to sleep, neither of them aware of the other's inner turmoil.

Chapter 2

January 1516
Greenwich Palace, London

As Wolsey had warned the king two years prior, Spain did indeed renege their pledge to join forces with England against France.

And as Henry now sat before the fire in his private chambers, staring drowsily at the dancing flames, he contemplated the recent developments that had come from this betrayal.

The war that Henry had hoped to wage on France did not come to pass, leaving England with no other option but to settle for peace.

In his frustration with Spain – as well as his need to settle the Anglo-French dispute now that there would be no war – King Henry VIII broke off the arrangement he had previously made for his younger sister, Mary Tudor, to marry Katherine of Aragon's nephew, Prince Charles of Castille. Instead, he organised for her to marry the old French King, Louis XII.

This way he had shown Spain that their betrayal had consequences, and that England would not be played for fools.

But his sister had not been best pleased.

How could you do this to me!? She had exclaimed at the announcement the previous year.

Her unladylike cry still echoed in Henry's ears.

However, after some time to regain her composure, and a moment of quiet deliberation with her close friend and sister-in-law, the queen, Mary Tudor had accepted her fate. But not without a condition of her own.

When the old man dies, she had told her king before her departure to France, *I want to marry a man of my choosing.*

Henry, as well as most of the court, had known of whom she spoke. His sister and the king's best friend, Charles Brandon, had been spending more and more time together: walking chaperoned in the palace gardens, or choosing one another for a merry dance during banquets. It was quite clear to see that they had fallen in love.

But Henry needed his sister to create alliances. As a princess, that was, quite literally, her entire purpose. Allowing her to marry a mere duke – even if he *was* Henry's dearest friend – would not do.

But he would hardly tell her as much.

You have my word, he had said instead, knowing it would never ensue anyway. For though King Louis XII was fifty-two years old, Mary, at eighteen, was young and no doubt fertile. She would surely be carrying the future Prince of France very soon; and therefore, be unable to leave France for many years.

Mary, taking her brother's word at face value, had broken into a wide grin, her pretty face beaming brightly and her eyes shining with thanks at her king. And she had travelled abroad, her marriage leading to a diplomatic union between England and France.

Their newfound peace did not last long, however, for King Louis XII died suddenly after just eighty-two days of wedded bliss to his new young queen. And Mary Tudor believed herself free to marry the man she truly loved.

Despite King Henry having given his verbal permission, he had ranted and raved over their secret wedding, even going so far as to threaten Charles with execution for his treachery.

In his benevolence, Henry had merely banished them from court instead, because deep down he knew that he was taking his mounting frustration towards his wife out on them – Katherine having suffered *another* stillbirth shortly after Mary's return from France.

But now, a year later, there was hope on the horizon once again. The couple had been forgiven and allowed to return to court, Henry's deceitful father-in-law King Ferdinand of Aragon was dead, and his queen was with child yet again.

King Henry VIII – and therefore his court – was merry once more.

A knock at the door roused Henry from his rambling thoughts then, and he sat up and cleared his throat, eager to admit who he knew was awaiting his word to enter.

For while all those recent positive developments gave the king much cause to be happy, it was his latest mistress which was to thank for the newfound spring in his step.

February 1516

"Just one more push, Your Highness, just one more," Bessie Blount promised her queen as she held her hand tightly and pressed a cloth to Katherine's damp brow.

Maud Green, Katherine's chief lady-in-waiting, flashed the young girl a disapproving look, Bessie realising that she ought not to promise Queen Katherine such a thing. For she, at fifteen-years-old, unmarried and childless, had absolutely no idea about childbirth.

Katherine puffed out short breaths in quick succession then as she knelt at the foot of the pallet bed, one hand wrapped around the birthing ropes, the other squeezing Bessie's small hand tightly.

There were midwives dotted all around the room, some fetching blankets, some whispering frantically in the corner, one of them attending the queen.

"What's wrong?" Queen Katherine asked now, sensing the midwives' worry like the vibrating of a busy beehive.

"Fetch Dr Vittoria," the older midwife called over her shoulder then, and Bessie watched them hurry out the door.

Bessie beamed at her queen, "He is coming, just as you requested."

Katherine smiled tightly at her youngest lady-in-waiting, trying to see the positive in her statement. For though she was correct that Katherine had – despite the midwives' horror – requested for a male doctor to aid her in this delivery, she also knew that their summoning of him meant they had encountered a complication.

Katherine's eyes stung to think that yet another of her babies would die before it'd had a chance to live. But she swallowed her burning tears and clenched her teeth as another contraction ripped through her just before Dr Vittoria was escorted into the room.

Minutes passed like hours, Katherine barely able to think straight as the pains coursed through her.

But with the physician's sage advice and the queen's determination, after three more strong pushes, her little baby was born.

And to the court and country's relief, it was born screaming.

"A girl! A useless girl, Charles!" King Henry bellowed in his private chambers, his pardoned friend being, once again, his most trusted confidant, "What am I to do with *that?*"

Charles cleared his throat, "The queen may have borne you a girl this time, but a healthy child by your legal wife is *good news*, Henry," he said, hoping to temper some of the king's disappointment.

"The princess will bring, with her future marriage, an alliance to strengthen England," Charles continued, "And at least with her successful birth you can rest assured that Queen Katherine *can* still bear you living children."

Henry had breathed in deeply at Charles' words, nodding his head in agreement as he had spoken.

"It has been so long since she has birthed a live child," Henry pondered, thinking of the son that had been born strong, only to die suddenly after just fifty-two days, "I was no longer sure Katherine had it in her."

Charles nodded his head slowly, aware of the king's struggles to sire an heir. And even now, with this girl, he had not succeeded in that goal.

"This is a victory, my king," he assured Henry, "Next time, no doubt, the queen will give you a son."

"Yes," Henry agreed, though he was already thinking of other things.

September 1518

Two years later, Henry VIII had another chance at obtaining an Anglo-French alliance, this time through his daughter, since his sister's marriage to the former King Louis XII had ended so suddenly three years earlier.
It was ironic, then, that it would be *another* Princess Mary Tudor who would be the new offering to France, Henry and Katherine having named their only surviving child after the king's favourite sister.
"I do not like this," Henry's Spanish Queen told him when it had been announced that their daughter, Mary, would be betrothed to the young French Prince.
As an *infanta* of Spain and daughter to the former rulers of Castille and Aragon, Katherine naturally resented France; and she had hoped that England and France would remain at each other's throats, as their history would suggest. But her father's betrayal some years ago had pushed England into France's arms, and the Spanish-born Queen of England could do nothing now but grin and bear it.
"I no longer care about what you do or do not like, Katherine," Henry slowly replied without looking up from the paperwork before him.
Throughout the years, the king's ardent love for his wife had finally faded; her continued inability to provide him with the *one thing* he needed as a monarch, being at the very forefront of his mind. And he no longer blamed himself for his part in having pushed her away by his own actions over the years.
After all, he was the king. And his right to do as he pleased was inherent in the title. His taking of mistresses, especially while the queen was with child – which Katherine, to her credit, had been a lot – was his God given *right*! And he had finally given up feeling ashamed for it. Especially since his newest conquest gave him so much joy…

Katherine did not reply, instead raising her chin and biting her tongue inside her closed mouth.

Henry looked up at her after a moment, standing tall and wonderful before the fireplace.

Despite his frustration with her, he could not deny that Katherine of Aragon was the most elegant and regal woman he had ever known – second only, perhaps, to his own lady mother, Queen Elizabeth of York, who had died when Henry was just ten.

Katherine possessed, without even trying, an aura of nobility that, while impressive and commanding, was not arrogant. She exuded sovereignty and allure, but without suggesting superiority.

It was a trait which – to this day – attracted Henry to her. At the very least it inspired his respect. But until she delivered him a healthy son, he would never again admit to it aloud.

He tore his gaze from her face and rested it upon the evident bump under her dress.

"How is my son?" he asked casually, though the question was as loaded as could be.

Katherine instinctively rubbed a delicate hand over her belly, "He is strong, my king," she offered, "His kicks are fierce and constant."

King Henry nodded once at the information, allowing his smile to show.

"I should hope so," he said, before returning to his paperwork and dismissing his queen with a wave of his hand.

That night – as he did most every night since Katherine's latest pregnancy – King Henry allowed himself to put aside his kingly duties, his troubles and his woes, by spending the night with the only person who could make him forget.

He had already had her once that night, both of them reaching climax quickly after he had pulled her into his chambers by the wrist and pressed her up against the wall, her skirts bunched around her waist as he'd pushed into her.

Now, as they both lay naked under the sheets in the king's bed, a slower form of lovemaking ensued. They took their time on their second coupling, the king making sure she finished first so that he could behold the look of raw desire flashing in her eyes.

He rolled off her when they were both spent, Henry wiping the sweat from his brow with the back of his hand.

After a moment, when their breathing had slowed, she moved towards him and rested her blond head on his chest, her hand playing absentmindedly with the red hairs on his abdomen.

"Do you think the queen knows?" she asked then, as she did every. Single. Time.

Henry rubbed a hand over his face. It was the *only* thing she did that irritated him: this show of guilt for 'betraying' her mistress.

"No," he replied curtly, though he was not entirely sure, "Nor would I care if she did."

He could feel the young woman thinking, her naked body having stiffened slightly as she draped over his chest.

Henry sighed audibly, making his opinion perfectly clear.

"If not you, I would have taken another," he admitted, realising too late that though he had meant to reassure her, his statement only reminded her of how replaceable she was.

She moved away, sat up with her back to him and began to pull her nightgown over her head.

"Forgive me, Your Highness," she said, "It was not my intent to spoil the evening."

Henry reached for her, rested his hand on her snow-white thigh, "Don't leave," he said, then grinned, "The night is young."

She turned to look upon her lover. His pale blue eyes were glinting mischievously, his thin lips pulled tight in a smug leer.

In contrast, what Henry saw when he looked upon her was an air of quiet devotion, and though her small, round mouth was set in an easy smile, her green eyes did not reflect in them the yearning he had hoped to invoke with his remark. Unable to look her in the eye any longer, he observed the splash of freckles on her small nose instead, then immediately wished he hadn't, for they only reminded him of Katherine's own.

He refused to feel guilty, however, and rolled away from his mistress with a scorned exhale, throwing his arm over his face.
Henry felt the mattress shift and heard the young woman padding around the room to gather her clothing. He looked up just as she reached for the doorhandle and pulled, her half-dressed form slipping out the room.

"Bessie, don't –" Henry called after her.
But she was already gone.

Chapter 3

October 1518

Bessie had great cause to be upset, for not only did the guilt of her betrayal to her queen weigh more heavily on her conscience with each sordid tryst, but she was now also hiding a terrible secret.
She had known of it for some time, though she had hoped it would resolve itself, for the shame it brought her to think her actions could cause Queen Katherine undue stress was too much to bear.
Yes, she eagerly and uncaringly lay with the king. Had secretly done so since she had reached her fourteenth birthyear. And each time, after hers and the king's carnal needs were fulfilled and she was returned to her senses, Bessie would often go back to her chambers with a churning stomach – shame bringing with it a touch of nausea.
But some weeks ago, Bessie had noticed that the usual nausea did not evaporate as it normally did the following day. Nor the next day, or indeed the week after.
And now, at eighteen-years-old, Bessie was not foolish enough to think that it was no more than a lingering bout of remorse.
This nausea had a different cause. One entirely separate from her mixed feelings over being the king's mistress, and yet completely related to it.
I think I'm with child, Bessie had informed her father, John Blount, when she could no longer deny it to herself, for a bump had begun to form.
John Blount wasted no time and immediately informed the king's right-hand man, Thomas Wolsey, of the development, so that the scandal may be kept secret. For the *last* thing his family needed was to be blamed for causing the queen distress. Not while she was potentially carrying the king's long-awaited son...

And so, it was arranged by Wolsey that Bessie be housed away from the prying eyes of the English court, at the Priory of St Laurence in Blackmore, Essex, to await the birth of the king's bastard child.

November 1518
Greenwich Palace, London

Thunder cracked loudly outside, lighting illuminating Queen Katherine's chambers in a brief and eery flicker.
The room was dimly lit, only the embers remaining in the fireplace, but as Katherine sat upright in bed, she could see the dark stain forming between her legs.
Katherine stared at it, frozen in horror as tears welled in her eyes, and she whispered to herself, "It's too soon…"
Her ladies-in-waiting awoke to the sound of their mistress' distress, and in moments the room was filled with noise and chaos. The midwives scurried about frantically, while Katherine's ladies huddled in the dark corners, their whispered prayers echoing throughout the room.
But there was no stopping what was happening, for the queen's baby was too eager to be born.
It easily slipped out of her with only two contractions, Katherine sobbing quietly into her cushions afterwards, her teeth chattering with terror and shock while the midwife bundled the tiny baby in blankets.
The room went deathly still, and though the storm outside had broken, the storm within Katherine was building greater with every second of silence as she awaited her child's first cry.
The child, wrapped in the old midwife's arms gave a little gurgle, then another, and Katherine felt her chest give way.
The queen knew the sound of death all too well, having lost child after child after…
Nobody made a sound as they watched the little newborn struggle to breathe, all of them feeling powerless, unable to do

anything to help it. The midwife looked up at Katherine, her tired eyes bloodshot with shared grief.

"Does Your Highness wish to hold her?" she asked, her voice cracking with emotion.

"Her?" Katherine whispered, but she knew it did not matter. Boy or girl, the child was not meant for this world, her body having expelled the poor babe too soon, like so many of her brothers and sisters before her.

The midwife nodded sombrely, "Let her pass in her mothers' arms," and she gently handed Katherine her dying daughter.

Katherine held her baby, then gently pressed a kiss to the top of her head, inhaling her unique newborn scent – the only thing Katherine would be able to keep locked in her memories once she would pass.

Then there was nothing left to do but to watch as the child's little chest shuddered with every inhale, each desperate gurgle more hopeless than the last.

And then, quite suddenly and all too soon, there was complete silence…and Katherine's last hope was gone from this world.

December 1518
Priory of St Laurence, Blackmore, Essex

Bessie learned of her queen's tragic loss from the king himself, who rode to Essex to seek comfort from the woman he now professed to love. Her.

It stung Bessie's heart to think of Queen Katherine feeling abandoned and alone during this time, but Bessie could do nothing but hold the king as he sniffled against her neck.

After a short while – in Bessie's humble opinion, a much too short a time to grieve the loss of a child – Henry pulled away and wiped a stray tear from under his eye, then turned a smiling face on her.

"How is my son?" he asked, placing his hands over her growing bump.

Bessie did not reply, unsure how blatantly she might dare to agree to the child's gender when there was no way of knowing until its birth.

"The babe is well," she said, settling for ambiguity.

Henry nodded, satisfied enough.

And Bessie wondered exactly why he even cared. Because boy or not, this child of theirs would never amount to anything.

For it would be illegitimate no matter what.

June 1519

Bessie Blount huffed and puffed all night, her pale face becoming clammy and red with exertion as she pushed and pushed, her body instinctively guiding her on what to do.

With her was her mother and two midwives, far less ado than when the queen gave birth, Bessie noted.

But she was pleased for it. For she could not imagine having a large audience during a time such as this, where she was vulnerable and in so much pain.

"I see the head," the young midwife informed the room, "One more push!"

Bessie did as she was instructed, and with a throaty grunt, she felt her baby being born.

Her mother, Katherine Blount, wiped her daughter's brow tenderly, kissing her cheek and whispering how proud she was of her.

But Bessie hardly heard her, for the room was suddenly filled with a shrill, ear-splitting screech.

The sound could break glass, she found herself thinking. And yet somehow it was the most wonderful noise Bessie had ever heard.

"What is it?" she heard herself asking, though her voice sounded faded, somehow reduced above the powerful cries of her child, as if her voice mattered far less now that it was born.

The midwife beamed at her, flashing crooked teeth.

"It is a son," she told Bessie, whose face twitched into disbelief.

"A boy?" she asked, sharing a look with her mother, then reaching out for her baby.

The midwife nodded as she handed over the shrieking bundle.

"A boy. Yes, indeed," she replied with an excited nod, "And a *strong* boy by all accounts!" The midwife grinned at the two mothers, then called over the child's intense cries, "The king will be extremely pleased!"

Greenwich Palace, London

The news of the king's son's birth swarmed like a plague of locusts all over London, and it was not long before all of England had heard the news.

The king – who after ten years of marriage to Katherine of Aragon had not yet managed to father a surviving son by her – immediately laid claim on the illegitimate boy.

In doing so, Henry hoped to prove to England – and the world – that he was still strong and virile, and that his lack of a male heir was not *his* doing, just as he had predicted for some time.

He named the babe after himself, of course, the tradition of naming a child after oneself being the ultimate seal of approval. And though he knew it would hurt his wife and queen, Henry could not stop himself from taking it one step further.

"This boy is proof," the king said to Cardinal Thomas Wolsey as they both stood on the king's balcony, overlooking the city.

"He is *proof* that the failing never lay with me! I *can* bear healthy sons!"

Though Wolsey knew that the king's firstborn son by Queen Katherine, Henry Duke of Cornwall, had also been born healthy, the Cardinal was not about to remind the king of that. The reason for the babe's sudden passing just weeks after his birth continued a mystery to this day, but he had not been born unhealthy, as the king was choosing to believe…

Henry went on excitedly, "I am acknowledging him as mine!" he grinned, "And I shall name him Fitzroy to emphasise his importance."

The Cardinal raised his eyebrows at the announcement.

"Fitzroy..." the older man repeated, *The son of the king.* Well, it certainly has a ring to it, Your Majesty. And his birth undoubtedly implies there may be male heirs to follow!"

Henry did not reply, simply staring down at the bustling city with a silly grin on his face.

After a pause, where Cardinal Wolsey considered taking his leave, the king suddenly spoke again.

It was merely a whisper, causing Wolsey to lean forward, "My liege?" he offered, in case the king had wanted him to hear.

Henry turned his beaming face at his advisor, his lips having stretched into a self-satisfied and cat-like leer.

"I knew it wasn't my fault."

September 1519

As Henry had expected, Katherine did not take the news well. What he hadn't expected, however, was how graciously she would contain her disappointment.

Upon the formal announcement of the boy's birth in the middle of a banquet, Katherine had merely risen from her seat at the high table and exited the great hall. Upon the child's christening as *Fitzroy*, she had simply jerked up her chin and congratulated the king with a bow of her head.

She had, of course, requested never to have to see her former lady-in-waiting again, an appeal which Henry gladly granted, if only to avoid unnecessary fuss. But other than that, Katherine of Aragon had maintained her composure as only a true queen could, and it sparked a flicker of admiration in Henry, a tiny burst of sympathy for the woman who had once been the love of his life. Only she could maintain that level of regality in the face of such obvious humiliation. And he almost – *almost* – believed that there may be hope for them yet.

The boy was christened and the king's right-hand man, Thomas Wolsey, was appointed as the child's godfather – another distinct indication that Fitzroy was of great importance despite his illegitimate status.

For a while, Henry's son was placed in the care of Lady Margaret Bryan, who was his other child, the Princess Mary's, governess. And the two half-siblings resided under the same roof at Hatfield House.

The little princess, at only three, may have been aware that this baby was not her full brother, but she remained ignorant of the strife his birth had caused between her parents. And so, when she looked upon him each morning, his big blue eyes searching the rooms and his pink mouth open in protest, Mary developed a kinship for the adorable bundle, happily referring to him as 'brother'.

However, this unusual turn of events did not sit right with the people or the nobles, such an obvious snub to their queen and their legitimate princess being too grotesque for them to stomach quietly. For to acknowledge an illegitimate male born child was one thing, but to arrange him in much the same way as one would a newborn Prince of England, that would not be accepted by the masses.

"I will allow him to return to his mother in the country," Henry proclaimed to his council one day, after hearing more outrage from the public for how he was presenting his bastard son, "Let the Blounts oversee his babyhood."

And so they did, Bessie Blount being most overjoyed to be reunited with her son, and her family more than happy to benefit from the king's continued devotion to his favourite mistress.

March 1520

King Henry continued to show favour to Bessie as the months went on, often visiting her and their son in the country, eager to watch the boy reach milestones his previous sons had never been lucky enough to achieve.

Henry would bring gifts for both Bessie and baby Henry whenever he would visit, making sure that the boy would grow up to understand that, while his father was not always present, that he was loved.

But in the spring of 1520 the king would learn that, as well as the many gifts, he had left behind a different kind of surprise.

"I am with child, Henry," Bessie informed her lover on one of his visits, the last time having been three months prior, when this child had been conceived.

Henry's red eyebrows shot up, "Another son?" he asked rhetorically, his hands reaching out to touch her belly.

As the last time when the king had assumed the child's gender, Bessie did not agree, but she smiled up at Henry, her cheeks flushed with joy.

Henry kissed her firmly on the lips, before turning to a now toddling baby Henry and lifting him into his arms.

"A brother for you, my dear boy!" Henry laughed triumphantly, his son screeching excitedly to be held aloft, his chubby hands clapping clumsily together.

With his mistress carrying another child by him, Henry found himself in a predicament.

For the purpose of preserving the life that was growing inside her, the king would not dare to lay with Bessie while she was with child. Nor did he have any inclination to share his queen's bed, for not only had the marital act lost its appeal, but he believed that Katherine, at thirty-five, was now at an age where conception was unlikely. And judging by her past experiences, even if it were to occur, chances were it would only end in heartbreak. And Henry did not care to even take the chance.

But the need to fornicate was never far from Henry's mind, and with his wife and mistress out of the running, he quickly set his sights on another beauty at court.

The girl was both young and pretty, had a lovely singing voice and a melodic laugh. She reminded Henry a lot of Bessie, before she had borne his children.

The king had known her since 1514, when she had been appointed as one of his sister's ladies-in-waiting during the time that she had been married to the old King Louis XII of France.

The young woman had remained in France following the death of King Louis and continued to attend the court of the new French king, Francis I, before returning to England in 1519.

Henry had heard the stories of her involvement with Francis I, had heard how the French King had apparently had her so often, he had nicknamed her 'his English Mare'.

But she was a married woman now, King Henry having personally attended her wedding at the invitation of her father, a courtier who was swiftly climbing the ranks within the English court.

She had looked beautiful on her wedding day, Henry now remembered as he considered his loverless status. Her husband was a *very* lucky man…

Francis I, too, had been a very lucky man…

And Henry decided to make it his personal mission to find out just *how* lucky they truly were.

September 1520

Since announcing her pregnancy to Henry, Bessie had seen less and less of him throughout the rest of the year, and as her belly grew, so did the time between his visits.

Her second child by the king was born exactly nine months after it was conceived, the midwife praising Bessie with a wide smile as she'd placed the meowling newborn in the crook of her arm.

"It is a girl," the midwife said, her smile never faltering. For why would it? Bessie's children could not inherit the throne,

no matter what gender they were born with. And so, in this case, a girl was not considered a disappointment.
Bessie knew this…she knew it.
But as the little girl nestled against her bosom, the young woman suddenly realised with a *pang* to her heart that her relationship with the king would now most certainly be over.

Chapter 4

April 1525
Kyme, Lincolnshire

Bessie had been right.
Ever since the birth of their second child five years earlier – who she had named Elizabeth, after herself – Henry VIII showed her no more interest. At least, not in the carnal sense.
Bessie, however, chose to believe that this had not been due to her birthing a daughter, but rather for the fact that the king had clearly fallen for a new lady at court. And Bessie had become no more than a cliché: out of sight, out of mind.
But could she even blame the king? When he had pretty ladies at his disposal day in, day out?
Bessie had been heartbroken for a while, sometimes having allowed herself to believe that she and Henry might have had a future. But it had been a folly, for no king would settle for a woman who could not give him legitimate children.
And – judging by Bessie's fertility – to have continued their relationship would have led to many more bastard children being born, bastard children the king likely would not have been able to continue to claim without causing civil unrest.
The lady that replaced Bessie, had, at least, already been married when King Henry began courting her. Meaning that any children borne by the king during *their* liaison would simply have been accepted as the de facto children of her husband, William Carey. Which was exactly what had happened in the case of the two children Mary Boleyn had birthed in the years that had followed. The years that she was actively laying with the king.
Bessie had understood the logic of it, but the initial rejection had stung all the same.
The king had acknowledged Bessie's son as his, at least. But to expect him to claim more bastards would not have sat well with

his queen or indeed his country. He'd needed to replace her with a woman who was already wed.

In the end, it had been for the best, however, for Bessie had been lucky enough to meet a good and honourable man in 1521 who had asked for her hand in marriage shortly thereafter and become her husband in March 1522 with the king's blessing. Gilbert Tailboys had accepted her despite her coloured past and accepted her children as though they were his own. He had even gone on to officially claim baby Elizabeth as his by giving her his surname, an honour which would spare her having to grow up a bastard.

He was one of Cardinal Wolsey's wards, and Bessie was not so naive to believe her marriage had not been suggested – or perhaps even arranged – by the king himself. But she was not displeased by the outcome. For, throughout their three-year marriage, Gil had proven himself worthy time and time again. And Bessie was happy.

In fact, she could not have asked for a kinder man! He had stepped into the role of father to her two young children effortlessly; and before long, nobody even remembered that little Elizabeth was not biologically his.

"How are my two beautiful ladies doing this fine morning?" Gil asked cheerfully now as he approached his little family at the breakfast table in their Kyme estates one cool spring morning.

He wore a bright smile on his face and an equally lively doublet on his torso, and Bessie frowned as he strode towards them to plant a kiss on her lips.

"What is the occasion, husband?" she asked while bouncing their first child, a boy, on her knee just as her five-year-old son Henry entered the hall.

She reached her free hand to her eldest child, and he walked into her embrace, his pensive face slightly downturned with tiredness.

"The king has summoned me," Gil informed his wife proudly, reaching over her to pluck a wedge of bread from her plate and shimmying their baby's chubby cheek with his finger.

The baby giggled and tried to grab his father's hand.

"For a private audience?" Bessie replied, and watched as his smiling mouth moved up and down as he ate.

"Indeed," he said around his mouthful, "And I have an idea that it is about your son."

At that, Bessie and Gil looked at Henry Fitzroy, as he looked up at them.

"What of him?" Bessie asked, her frown deepening between her light eyebrows.

Gil walked around the table, tickled little Elizabeth's tummy as he sat down beside her. The four-year-old girl squirmed, giggling.

"You remember the king's accident last year?" he asked.

Bessie nodded, her stomach clenching with the memory, "Yes, the joust, the lance to his face when he forgot to lower his visor…What about it?"

Gil sighed at the dryness of the bread and waved a servant over, "Fetch me some wine," he told the girl, before turning back to his wife.

"He has had another close encounter with death."

Bessie gasped in horror, "Is the king alright?" she asked, and immediately wished she hadn't sounded so desperate to know. She looked down at the baby on her lap then, pretended to wipe drool off his chin.

But Gil did not flinch at her reaction, unperturbed by her past. He never did judge her for it. And that in itself made her feel even worse for still caring for the king.

Gil nodded, "King Henry is well," he ensured her, "But he almost drowned. He attempted to cross a trench by pole vaulting it and fell into the muddy ditch, headfirst no less."

At that, little Henry cracked a smile, and Gil shot him a companionable wink.

Bessie noticed this slight exchange between the two, "Do not smirk at that!" she hissed, "He is the king. He is your father, Henry!"

Henry dropped his head in shame, but Gil could tell a small smile lingered.

"Come now, Bessie," Gil laughed as he brushed his chestnut hair off his forehead, "We are not finding humour in the accident, merely in…well, the nature of it."

Bessie shook her head, took a sip of her small ale.

The servant returned with Gil's wine and poured him a cup. He nodded at the girl in thanks.

"Pole vaulting over a ditch," Gil repeated to himself with a lingering smile, shaking his head, "Whyever he did not simply walk around the damned thing I will never understand."

He took a gulp of his wine.

Henry and his little sister Elizabeth had begun talking quietly to each other, bored of the adult conversation. Henry was laughing as he spoke, his face brighter than when he first appeared in the doorway, his sister and he always having had a beautiful bond.

"But what has all this got to do with our son?" Bessie asked after a moment of watching the children.

Gil swallowed and smacked his lips in appreciation of the wine, then put the cup down before him and observed his lovely wife. When she continued to only stare at him with the same question on her face, Gil grinned and leaned forward to take her hand in his.

"Well, my dear," he said, "I can only guess that the king has had a terrifying wake-up call as to his own mortality, and that he's considering what alternative possibilities there may be for the future of England."

He and Bessie turned to look at little Henry again as he giggled and chatted with Elizabeth.

"A future that may very well involve his only surviving son."

The two children ran through the kitchen gardens, heady with the scent of rosemary and fennel, before bursting out into the field behind their house.

Little Henry turned around to face his four-year-old sister and grinned. Now that they were outside, they could be as noisy as they'd like. The baby would never hear them from all the way out here.

"Come on," Henry insisted, waving his arm over his shoulder to prompt Elizabeth along.

The girl picked up her skirts and hurried to keep up with her big brother, the two of them sharing a love for the outdoors, as well as spending time with one another.

It wasn't the best day to be outside, April having brought with it a pretty-much constant drizzle. But the children would not be deterred, and they ran through the gauzy air on their way to their favourite tree: a stunted silver birch tree that had, over the decades, sprouted the best branches for climbing.

"Here," Henry said once they reached the base of the tree, stooping down and twining his fingers together to produce a step to help his little sister climb up, "You first, so that I can catch you if you fall."

Elizabeth giggled, her baby voice still very much present, "I won't fall," she promised.

"Not too high," Henry warned, watching her plant her feet on the first few branches, then following carefully behind.

Together, they climbed, Henry enjoying the wet bark under his palm.

"Look, Henry," Elizabeth trilled, "a nest."

Henry, having come up beside her on a long and sturdy branch, peered at the collection of twigs, a lone fluffy feather moving in the breeze.

"It's empty," he said, then plucked the feather and pocketed it.

Soon they were high enough to be hidden among the leaves, and with Elizabeth hugging the trunk, the sibling duo sat side by side on a thick branch, their legs swinging companionably.

Through the gaps in the foliage, they could see their home, and the window at which they knew their mother would be sitting as she sang to the baby, their new brother.

"Do you think mama will call for us soon?" Elizabeth asked Henry.

The boy shook his head, "Not until baby George has slept."

Elizabeth turned, began picking at the bark of the tree.

"What is it?" Henry asked then, noticing her mood shift to suddenly match the weather.

"It makes me sad sometimes," the girl admitted.

"What does?"

She shrugged, "The baby."

Henry frowned, his eyes shining with confusion, "But why?"

She did not reply, turning a smiling face to him instead, "Do you think you will meet the king soon?" she said, changing the subject easily, as only children could.

"The king?" Henry repeated, "He is my father, you know?"

Elizabeth nodded, though she pursed her lips as if she didn't really.

"Will you bring me back something when you go to see him?" she asked.

Henry giggled, "I'll bring you back a diamond," he said.

Elizabeth laughed, then wobbled on the branch. Instinctively, her brother reached out a hand to steady her.

"Careful!" he said, pressing his mouth into a stern line, "If you get hurt, you know we won't be allowed back up here."

Elizabeth looked down at the grass below them, "Maybe we should go back down?"

Henry shook his head, "Don't fret," he said, "I've got you."

And then, just to make sure she knew he meant it, he reached inside his pocket and pulled out the fluffy birds' feather and tucked it behind her ear.

"Here," he said, "So that you will fly even when I'm not around to catch you."

Greenwich Palace, London

"I wish to elevate my son," King Henry informed his advisors during one of the regular council meetings, "It is already arranged, Wolsey and I have discussed it at length."
At the mention of his name, the cardinal bowed his head at his master.
"I no longer expect male heirs by the queen," the king continued, "And therefore I find it only right that my surviving son be recognised. I cannot name him my successor…as several of you have pointed out, it would lead to civil unrest."
Thomas More, the king's friend and one of his most diligent and trusted advisors, nodded as he remembered the private conversation he and Henry had had the month before, when he had set his king straight in sending his legitimate daughter to preside over the Prince's Council in Wales, rather than his illegitimate son.
"The people would never have accepted it had you sent the boy to Ludlow instead of the Princess Mary," More concurred.
Henry nodded and exhaled loudly, "No, you are right, Thomas. And I have accepted it. My daughter – shall be my heir."
More and several council members nodded their heads in admiration, some even exchanging smiles.
Henry noticed their wordless interactions, irked to see their easy acceptance of the princess, for he had not yet *fully* recognised it as his only option, despite what he had announced.
Henry VIII had formulated a plan. But he realised now, as his advisors showed genuine contentment with the idea of his daughter as his successor, that it would likely take many more years to change the noblemen's minds as to his son's importance.
He could only hope that his intent to elevate Fitzroy would one day lead to theirs – and the people's – approval of him. Because leaving the throne to his daughter…well, quite frankly, it made his stomach turn.

"Nevertheless," Henry continued then, clapping his hands together once and bringing their attention back to his son and away from his daughter, "As I was saying: I wish to make use of my boy if he is to be my only living son."
The king leaned back in his seat at the head of the council table and snapped his fingers at a servant in the shadows.

"Fill our cups," the king ordered the young man, before looking his councilmen in the eyes, "We shall be here for a while."

June 1525
Windsor Castle, London

In just a few days' time, Henry Fitzroy would turn six-years-old, and to commemorate that milestone from child to young man, he, his mother and stepfather were summoned to court.

"Your father has big plans for you, my boy. He has elected you as Knight of the Garter – the highest honour!" Gil Tailboys told him, an excited grin brightening his face, and Henry looked to his mother to see if she, too, felt excited for what was to come. For though Henry did not understand what his stepfather had said, he knew it was a big deal.
The castle was vast, to say the least.
Henry poked his head out the open window of their carriage, his golden red hair wisping into his pale blue eyes, and he gasped at the sight of it as it grew larger with their approach. The gardens surrounding the outer courtyard were primly trimmed and kept, hedges shaped in all different sizes and figures, rose bushes blooming vibrantly in their assorted beds. Their carriage stopped and they climbed out, Henry's stepfather first, offering his mother a smile and a sturdy hand to help her climb out, then Henry followed behind. He looked up at the castle.

"Wow," he breathed.

To Henry, its spires appeared tall enough to touch the clouds, and the many windows were so large he thought that surely giants lived within the confines of the building.

And suddenly, as the castle loomed over him, he felt a physical kind of dread budding within him. Right at the base of his throat.

St George's Chapel, Windsor Castle

Little Henry had always known that Gil Tailboys was not his real father, and that he was the bastard son of the King of England.

In fact, young Henry's earliest memory was that of a red-headed man wearing a bejewelled jacket holding him aloft and grinning proudly up at him as he giggled, before squeezing him tightly in his strong arms. Only the image of the king measured up to that memory, and as the years went on, he had heard enough conversations to understand that he and his sister were the king's illegitimate children, born before their mother had married the man who would raise them.

But Henry had not seen his father in quite some time now and had no fresh memories of him.

Following their move to Kyme in Lincolnshire when he was just three years old, Henry had been tutored by his own mother – just as she herself had been tutored by hers. According to her, Henry was a 'bright young boy' and an 'eager learner', and it always filled his chest with joy to hear his mother praise him, especially when she did so in front of his stepfather, who Henry had grown to love as though he were his true parent.

But now, as little Henry awaited his cue to enter the large wood doors to St George's Chapel to be installed as Knight of the Garter, he could feel his hands beginning to sweat. And in that moment he did not feel bright or eager. He only felt very, very small.

Henry wore a cloak around his skinny shoulders bearing his own coat of arms, incorporating the royal lions and *fleur-de-*

lis, and a red and gold cap over his auburn hair. Outwardly, he looked as if he belonged among the nobles and bishops that surrounded him, all ready to take part in the procession, but in the privacy of his own mind, Henry had never felt so completely out of his depth.

The procession began with the sounding of trumpets, and the large doors opened so effortlessly that Henry found himself wondering yet again if giants resided in the castle.

As the head of the chivalric Order of the Garter, his father – the majestic King Henry VIII dressed in his rich robes and bejewelled fingers and clothes – would enter last, bringing up the rear while the nobles lead the way in a slow and steady march, with little Henry in among them.

Inside, the chapel was intimidating and the young boy all but gawked at the splendid sight of it. On both sides were windows so large they reached the high stone ceilings, which were intricately designed with folds and loops so meticulous it made Henry's mind whirr. But most daunting of all was the colourful stained-glass window on the far wall, each panel featuring important figures of the ages: kings, saints, princes, knights, popes – all men of great merit!

And to stand before them made Henry feel suddenly grossly out of place, awkward and – truthfully – a little frightened.

The whole event went by in a blur, the young boy unsure of what was expected of him, surrounded by great men saying great things, speeches which he hardly understood though he had tried to pay careful attention. But worst of all was when he was abruptly engulfed by a weighted silence, and he'd looked up to see everyone staring at him expectantly. He'd realised, too late, that the king had spoken directly to him, and his cheeks had flushed hot-red to notice his mishap. But to his relief, it had not halted the ceremony.

Perhaps his input was not *that* important in the turning of the cogs, after all.

When the day was finally over and he was allowed to retire to his chambers with his mother and stepfather, Henry took to running ahead and dragging his mother behind him by the hand, so anxious was he to distance himself from the stifling social event.

"Will we be able to return home soon, mama?" he asked as soon as they were safely within the confines of their chambers. Bessie smiled down at her firstborn. She noticed that his lisp was more prominent than usual, as she assumed it would be, tiredness always having accentuated the adorable little trait in him.

She removed her fancy gloves, then cupped her son's still-plump cheeks. His babyhood may be over, she thought, but the wonderfully angelic face remained. And she wondered then, with a pinch of her heart...*for how much longer?*

"No, my darling," she told him, "You are invited to attend court for a little spell yet," she looked up at her husband then, "Though I believe I myself have outstayed my welcome, judging by the queen's expression during the ceremony."

Gil's brows creased for a moment when they locked eyes, and an entire conversation was had right before Henry's eyes without so much as a spoken word, as only adults could do.

Henry looked back and forth between them, his red eyebrows twitching as he tried not to cry.

"But, why?" the boy asked, returning to the only scrap of information he had gathered from their private interaction.

Gil sat down at a seat by the fire and pulled off his boots.

"This title you received today," he explained, "It is but the first of many you shall be granted, my boy."

Henry looked over at his stepfather, his blue eyes wide with trepidation.

"Will there be more ceremonies and processions like today?" he said, his little voice wobbling, his lisp making it hard to pronounce the bigger words.

Gil grinned at Henry, hoping to afflict his stepson with his own enthusiasm, if only to spare him from his angst. He didn't like to see this boy, whom he loved like a son, feeling so uneasy.

"Oh, Henry," he sighed with faux cheer, "Today was nothing compared to what is yet to come."

Bridewell Palace, London

Not since the 12th century, when Henry II had made William Longsword Earl of Salisbury, had a King of England raised his illegitimate son into the peerage.
And yet it was happening once again, when another event took place to elevate Henry Fitzroy higher still.
The hall in Bridewell Palace was richly decorated, with various members of the court and the nobility in attendance to pay witness to Fitzroy's elevation. Among them were several bishops as well as dukes, earls, lords and ladies of the realm.

"There are currently but two dukes in all of England, my boy," Gil told his stepson in a hurried whisper, in the hope of explaining some of what was happening. He pointed out two men dressed in their finest.

"Thomas Howard the Duke of Norfolk, and Charles Brandon the Duke of Suffolk. They each have an important bond with the king."
Henry nodded his head as if he understood, taking in the images of the two noble men within the mumbling crowd. They appeared larger than life, in their robes and jackets of cloth of gold and furs draped over their shoulders despite the warm weather.
During the first ceremony that day, the young boy was created Earl of Nottingham, attended by a man called Henry Percy, Earl of Northumberland, who carried the sword of state before him.
Little Henry had been instructed to kneel before the king, which he did now with all the composure he could muster, as another great man, Thomas More, read out the patents of nobility. The words did not compute in Henry's mind, so focused was he on not bursting into flames as hundreds of eyes watched him carefully. And as More's voice droned on,

Henry's heart beat so fast that everything sounded as if under water.

After what felt like an age, the King of England bid Henry to rise, and upon doing so, he had somehow become an Earl.

Apparently, it was as simple as that.

But the ceremony was not yet completed, and the onlookers then watched as the boy exited the hall as he'd been previously instructed to, then re-entered moments later dressed in an ermine robe and flanked by England's two dukes.

They made a dazzling entrance into the hall, the young boy – a replica of the king in his youth – sandwiched between the two great men. No one, except perhaps the boy's stepfather, noticed or even cared that the child was still utterly terrified. And Gil thought, as he watched from among the crowd, that the grand robes and pompous ceremony aside, the boy bore the face of a deer caught in a trap. But he could do nothing but offer his young lad a comforting smile from among the sea of faces, reassuring him that it would all be over soon.

Behind them, as they walked steadily ahead, the Earl of Northumberland carried Fitzroy's robes and, once again, the young boy knelt before his majestic father.

This time when he rose to his feet, Henry Fitzroy was proclaimed the Duke of Richmond and Somerset, which he later learned was a double dukedom, one that would outrank the only other two dukes in existence within England, the very two who stood at either side of him now with cool and collected smiles upon their faces.

And so he, a boy of six years of age, born out of wedlock – a mere *bastard* – was now the highest-ranking member of the English nobility, second only in status to that of his half-sister Princess Mary herself.

And, for some reason he could not understand, since he had done nothing worth applauding, the crowd erupted in celebration.

"The use of the Duchy of *Somerset* as the boy's Dukedom was not accidental," Henry Fitzroy heard one of the courtiers telling another beside him during the banquet that had followed, "It is a well-known fact that the Beaufort's eldest child was John Somerset, a royal bastard who had been legitimised following his parents' adultery and subsequent marriage."

"You think the king plans to do the same? To legitimi –"

The man beside him elbowed the other in the ribs suddenly then, and they both looked towards Henry.

Then the courtiers took a bite of the meat in their hands and continued to talk quietly and with full mouths, after which Henry did not hear any more of what they were saying. Not that it made much of a difference, as the young boy hadn't understood a single word the men had spoken anyhow.

Henry may have been titled an Earl, a Duke, a Knight of the Garter. But that didn't make him any less of a small child. And these adult matters were as yet impossible for him to truly comprehend.

Following the feast, there was a lavish masquerade, one which the king himself partook in, and this – *finally* – Henry could enjoy.

"How do you feel, son?" said his stepfather as Henry clapped joyfully to the music and the dancers.

Gil sat down beside him as the performers frolicked on the dancefloor and a collective *Hey!* was called out in time with the beat of the tune.

Henry smiled at Gil's use of the term he had always applied to him – *son*, as though he were his own. But, as Henry looked up at the king dancing among the masked courtiers now – the father who had this day given him so much – for the first time, it felt wrong.

"Tired," the boy admitted with a weary smile, "It is as though the day will never end."

Gil breathed a small laugh and followed his stepson's gaze at the dancers, the music curling around them like smoke.

"It will end soon," he assured him with a nod.

Henry looked up at Gil, the man who had been his father in ways that his *true* father would never be. One who had been there during tantrums, falls and scrapes, nightmares. One who had granted Henry's sister Elizabeth his own surname, and who would have likely granted him the same honour if Henry had needed it.

What he felt for his stepfather was warm and safe, and no amount of grandeur could eclipse that. Could it?

"And then what?" the boy asked, his voice sounding suddenly smaller than ever before, "What will happen when I awake on the morrow?"

Gil pressed his lips together into a tight smile.

"Tomorrow, my dear boy," he said, with a hint of both sadness and glee, "Tomorrow you shall embark on a new life. One that will catapult you to the heavens. One your mother and I could never even have dreamed of giving you."

"And you'll come with me?" the boy hitched, already knowing the answer, "You, and mama? Elizabeth and baby George?"

Gil cocked his head to one side, then looked back at the merry court before them, "I'm afraid not. Your life and ours part ways for now. You have been given an incredible opportunity, my son. And we must all be strong now, so that you may one day reach for the stars."

Chapter 5

July 1525
Durham Place, London

Following Henry's elevation, he was separated from his family, given his own household of staff, and moved to inhabit in one of Cardinal Thomas Wolsey's residences, where he would commence a more suitable education befitting his new status.

Henry had been distraught to leave his mother, sister and stepfather, but also glad to be able to move out of the public eye of the court following the many ceremonies. He was not used to being constantly ogled and praised, and having eyes on him at all times made him uncomfortable. But it had been a confrontation between the king and his queen shortly after receiving his title of Duke which had caused Henry the most unease.

The queen had apparently – though Henry had only found out through court gossip – made her resentment of his earldom and dukedom very clear to the king, going so far as to proclaim that she was 'dissatisfied with it'.

Henry had not stayed at court long enough to witness his father's reaction, but he later heard that the king had blamed three of the queen's ladies for encouraging her and dismissed them from court there and then.

Henry did not fully understand the significance of it all, but he could sense the tension in the air. Even as he resided miles away from Greenwich Palace.

But though he was no longer in the midst of the English court, the ceremonies did not stop, and in the weeks that followed Henry was further created Warden General of the Northern Marches – just as King Henry VIII himself had been at his age – as well as Lord High Admiral of England.

None of these titles held any meaning for the boy, however, who was frankly too confused to remember which was which and what was what. But if he understood correctly, these new titles were of the same level of honour as that of the Princess Mary being sent to preside over the Prince's Council in Wales. Whatever that meant.

Henry had no idea what his responsibilities now were, or what was expected of him – for surely all these titles meant he now had something to do…?

Would people refer to him as Duke? As General? As Earl?

He could not even begin to guess. Was he even still Henry?

It was all too much, and the young boy would go to bed each night feeling too heavy in his little body, and too tired to even waste energy on crying for his mother.

August 1525

"That infernal lisp better be something you outgrow, my Lord Richmond!"

That was what he was now referred to as: Richmond.

He was no longer Henry – at least not to greater men – and he was no longer a child.

As promised, a tutor was appointed to him with his new royal status, one that would no doubt lead him to a higher understanding of the world. But for the first few weeks, all they focused on was correcting Henry's 'appalling pronunciation of Latin'.

"Again," his tutor, Palsgrave – who had formerly been Princess Mary's tutor – commanded.

They had been at it for hours. At least, it *felt* like hours…

But Henry bent his head over the textbook and licked his dry lips in the hope of controlling his tongue.

He had never been aware that he spoke with what Palsgrave called a 'lisp'. His mother had never pointed it out, neither had his stepfather. Perhaps they, too, had never noticed?

More likely, they had not minded…

But Palsgrave...he seemed to mind a lot.

"*Pater nothhter...qui ethh in...caelithh –*"

"No, no no no," Palsgrave interrupted, slamming his wooden cane on the table.

Henry jumped at the sound, as he did every time.

"The tongue," the old man said again, his free hand curled into a claw, "Control the tongue!"

Henry pressed his lips together tightly and bit the inside of his cheek. He could feel his eyes stinging with tears, so he squeezed them tightly shut. It would only make it worse if he was seen to cry.

"We should go hawking instead!" a voice beside him piped up then.

Following Henry's elevation, George Blount – his mother's youngest brother – had had the lucky honour of joining Henry's household and thereby attending the king's son's lessons. He was older than Henry by five years but of lower rank, meaning that even to receive an education to that of a six-year-old would-be prince, was far better than any learning he would ever have received in different circumstances.

Henry had known George since before he could remember, and though he was his uncle, the boys got on like cousins, their similar age bonding them thusly.

Henry flashed George a grateful look then, as Palsgrave shot his attention to the older boy and away from him, and he was able to dash the tears away with his sleeve when no one was looking. Then he cleared his throat to agree with his friend.

"Hawking!" Henry called with a grin, "Yes, indeed, let us do that!"

Palsgrave's face was a picture: his mouth open in halted protest, his bushy eyebrows taut with surprise. And before he could gather his words to deny them, the two young boys scurried out the door, giggling as they went.

"You will get in trouble," Henry told George once they had escaped, skidding to a halt in the courtyard.

George shrugged, "So will you."
Henry couldn't help himself, and his face relaxed into a smug smile, "Unlikely."
George laughed as they walked around a corner and past a group of robed men.

"Of course, *my lord*," he said teasingly, "No one shall ever punish you again."
Henry grinned, "Is it my fault I am of such import?"

"I guess not," George replied, looking down at the ground as they walked, "But it would be foolish of you not to take advantage of it. While you can."

"Like you are?" Henry argued jokingly, elbowing his uncle in his skinny ribs.

"Oh-ho!" George laughed, lifting his hands up in mock defeat, "You caught me out, *nephew*! Your luck is my gain, and so on and so forth."
Henry laughed as they exited the manor, "Well then, *uncle*, let's make the most of it before Palsgrave tells my lord father and puts an end to the fun!"

But Palsgrave did not inform the king, choosing instead to write to the boy's mother, Bessie Tailboys, of how atrociously she had educated him.

"He says he can hardly speak Latin," Bessie blubbered to Gil one evening upon receiving the harsh letter from her son's new tutor, "he chastises me for allowing his lisp to control him, and for failing to teach him the basics of prayer!"
Gil took the letter from her and without so much as a glance at it he tossed it into the fire. The flames *puffed* it into ash within seconds.

"He is but taking his frustration out on you because he cannot scold the boy too roughly without being held accountable by the king," her husband explained, then took her into his arms, "Be glad you are receiving the brunt of it and not Henry."

"Do you really think so? Or is this a clever ruse to calm me?" Bessie sobbed.

Gil smiled at her, "I would not lie to you."

Bessie sighed and nodded against his chest, "I know," she said, "But I cannot help but feel accountable. He was my responsibility."

"And you did a fine job, my dear," Gil murmured into her neck, his hands fumbling with her hood, "Henry is a good boy, with a big heart and a kind soul," he said in between kissing her jawline, "Let the old grumble send you letters. I have no doubt that soon, they shall be nothing but praising of our boy's talents."

Bessie allowed his words and tenderness to soothe her. And before she knew it, she was no longer thinking about Palsgrave and his unfair criticisms, but of her loving husband and the warmth of his hands on her skin.

December 1525

Young Henry's first Christmastide without his family went better than he had expected it would.

To celebrate the twelve days of Christmas, he had been invited by his father to attend court, leaving Durham Place for the first time since his elevation.

Greenwich Palace had felt magical upon his arrival, the young boy looking around in awe, his mouth hanging slightly open. Decorated with holly, ivy, mistletoe, laurel, candles and ribbons, the king's court was transformed.

Throughout the celebratory period, lessons were put on hold, replaced with much feasting, dancing, and entertainment, and Henry was often called upon to spend private time with his father the king, where they would play chess or cards in the great hall.

The air hung thick with the wonderful scent of Christmas: wassail – hot ale infused with roasted apples – and pomanders – oranges studded with cloves – wafting into Henry's nostrils at every turn.

He felt warm and happy every single day.

That is, until the New Year's celebrations, where the king and queen gave and received gifts.

"To my own jewel!" the king called after having received gifts of money, spices, and paintings, and presenting the queen and their daughter Princess Mary with jewels and bolts of cloth of gold.

Henry noticed many courtiers looking directly at him then.

Was *he* the king's jewel?

He stepped forward.

"I gift you a gold collar and a pearl!"

Henry heard gasps from among the crowd of courtiers, some smiling at the boy, others looking away almost sheepishly. Henry frowned, failing to understand why they looked uncomfortable.

"Thank you, Your Highness," the boy said with a bow, concentrating hard on keeping his tongue behind his teeth as he spoke, just as Palsgrave had instructed.

King Henry laughed, "Son," he called, "No need for such formality."

Henry's cheeks blushed, whether from the mishap, the people watching him, or the two cups of wassail he had had, he did not know.

"Thank you, Lord Father," he corrected, accepting his gifts gratefully.

He stepped down from before the thrones then, suddenly eager to get out of the spotlight, when he caught the queen staring at him in a most morose manner. Quite unbefitting the merriment of the day, he thought.

Perhaps she is unwell?

Her contempt made the boy stumble as he returned to his place among the crowd and he quickly cast his gaze to the ground when he noticed some others, the queen's ladies and the Princess Mary especially, glowering at him.

Until that moment, he'd quite forgotten how much his mere existence appalled many of the court.

He swallowed hard and took a step further back to hide behind the other courtiers. And just like that, he was reminded of where he stood.

February 1526

Henry had been glad to return to Durham Place after the festivities. The merriment had been enjoyable, the celebrations and the palace breathtaking. But there could be too much of a good thing…and when he had felt the shift in ambience, little Henry was glad to see the end of the Christmastide.

Business was returned to normal, and though the break had been needed, Henry was eager to return to his lessons. He enjoyed learning, despite Palsgrave's adamance that his understanding was substandard, as well as his apparent dislike of the boy.

By now, Henry – at almost seven years old – had lost his two top milk teeth, which Palgrave had grinned widely about, saying that it would likely aid in the disappearance of his lisp once his adult teeth grew in.

But Palsgrave never did last long enough as Henry's tutor to find out if his theory was correct, for after just six months, he was replaced with another.

Richard Crooke was much more lenient on the young boy, praising him on his advanced reading and translating, when Palsgrave had always deemed him behind on those very topics. And for that, at least, Henry was thankful to his new tutor.

"I shall write to the king of your excellent capabilities, my Lord Richmond," Crooke would smile at Henry, "It is a marvel that one so young could achieve so much in such little time."

George would tease Henry about Crooke's praise, however, claiming that it was 'nothing but arse-kissing' and only to embellish his own standing with the king.

"He's blowing smoke up his own backside, he is," George said one evening after their daily lessons, where Henry was praised for having the most basic of knowledge.

The two boys were sitting cross-legged in the gardens, absentmindedly tossing pebbles into the fountain as the last rays of sunlight dipped below the horizon. There was a frog sitting on the edge of the fountain which the boys were idly aiming for, shielded slightly by the growing twilight. It was croaking peacefully into the air, minding its own business as they talked.

Henry did not know how to respond to his friend when he said such things. It made his stomach twist with embarrassment, for surely it meant that he thought Henry was, in fact, not as clever as their new tutor professed.

Did George think him *dumb*, then?

The thought made Henry's skin prickle with shame. He couldn't stand the idea of being laughed at by his friend, or anyone for that matter.

In his humiliation, a bubble of anger burst to the surface, and Henry tossed the pebble in his hand with a little more force, zeroing in on their oblivious target.

The sound of the frog croaking raggedly then made Henry perk up and George froze mid-throw. The two boys looked at each other.

"Did I hit it?" Henry asked as a slow, involuntary grin spread over his face.

George scoffed a disbelieving laugh and scrambled up to investigate, Henry following behind.

As George squinted into the darkening waters, the sun now having dipped behind the trees, Henry walked around the perimeter of the fountain.

"Do you see anything?" he whispered to George, though he was not sure why.

"Nothing," George replied. Then, "Ah-ha!" he called, before stretching his arm into the fountain and pulling the limp frog out by its foot.

"You *did* get it!" George exclaimed with amazement, wriggling the knocked-out animal about.

Henry's eyes went wide with incredulity and his mouth spread into a gap-toothed beam.

"Maybe Crooke is right after all," George laughed then, his tone teasing, "Maybe you are exceptional..."

Henry's red eyebrows twitched, his delight immediately knocked back to think of his supposed failings yet again, as well as uncertain how this related to his ability – or lack thereof? – in the classroom.

Again, humiliation warmed his skin. He did not like to be sneered at by George, regardless of their friendship – or perhaps because of it.

It made him feel inferior, ridiculed, silly. Like a child. And he was no longer a child. Not according to his father – the *king!*

The shame began to burn the tips of his ears as his thoughts churned out of control.

But while George continued to poke and prod the unconscious animal in his hand, occasionally looking up at his young nephew with an amused laugh, Henry noticed something else in his friend's eyes. The mockery and sarcasm aside, Henry could sense a genuine admiration as George wiggled the poor creature. He was clearly fond of Henry's skilful aim.

And a wave of realisation slowly swelled within Henry, one that flooded his previous chagrin.

Maybe he was not meant for the classroom, for textbooks, Latin and *pronunciation*.

Maybe...it was Henry's physical abilities and outdoor pursuits that would see him recognised.

March 1526
Sheriff Hutton Castle, Yorkshire

With Henry Fitzroy's new titles and education came duties befitting his station, and that included relocating when the king needed him to.

The Northern counties had recently become noticeably unruly following Henry's elevation and the king's snubbing of his wife, the Northerners' passion to defend their beloved queen causing somewhat of a stir. To avoid their discontent from boiling over, the king had decided to restore the Council of the North – an administrative body first set up in 1484 to improve control over Northern England. He selected some of his best advisors to establish the Council and appointed his son – the very cause of the Northerners' disgruntlement – as Lord President of the Council, thereby granting his son yet another title and more power, as well as reminding the North of who was in charge.

To look the part, King Henry had given his son money for new clothes and granted him men from his own King's Council to travel north with him for the occasion.

Henry Fitzroy – now dubbed Richmond – who was by now a skilled rider, chose not to travel in the litter provided for him for the journey. Instead, he rode alongside the men of the council on his own gelding, looking majestic and grown, though he was not yet seven-years-old. And, as Henry had predicted, it granted him much praise and admiration from the nobles.

His duties while residing in Yorkshire, he was later told, would be largely ceremonial however, such as receiving local dignitaries. While the real decision-making would be left to the King's Council. Young Henry would therefore, with his mere presence, be no more than a representative of the king himself and would not *actually* be made to make any decisions, or even be asked his opinion.

That was somewhat of a relief, thought the young boy, for though he felt proud to have received yet another honour, he continued completely clueless as to what was required of him. But Henry was never bored, for he was always busy with other pursuits, activities and studies befitting his age and company.

Along with his new residence and title, Henry's household had gained another addition: a boy of closer age to him than George, and one who would swiftly prove himself a jolly companion.

His name was Henry Howard.

"Call me Hal," he had said upon introduction, as he'd stuck out his hand for Henry and George to shake. Henry had done so gladly, a grin spreading across his face to take in the new boy's mischievous smirk.

He was the eldest son of Thomas Howard, 3rd Duke of Norfolk – who Henry remembered from his elevation into dukedom – and first cousin to King Henry's former mistress Mary Boleyn.

"What is there to do around here for fun?" Hal had asked on that first day, flashing crooked front teeth.

Their tutor, Richard Crooke had *tutted* loudly. He already had his hands full with George, who enjoyed nothing more than to coax young Henry from the classroom.

April 1526

They ran down the main staircase as quietly as they could, to avoid their tutor's wrath. Crooke was far more lenient than Palsgrave, but George's continued bad influence on Henry and Hal had led to quite a few scoldings over the past few weeks.

Twelve-year-old George stifled a laugh at the sound of little Henry puffing behind him, Hal hot on his heels.

"Give it to me!" Henry hissed.

Turning around, George noticed the younger boy's face was pink with effort and perhaps more than a little angry that he had swiped Henry's Latin book from his desk before their escape. He flashed Hal a look but noticed straight away where the new boy's loyalties lay.

George looked back at little Henry. It appeared that while his nephew did not mind skiving, he did not wish for any harm to come to his precious workbooks, no matter how much he tried to pretend that he cared more for outdoor pursuits.

"Come get it," George replied, raising his arm high above his head.

Henry narrowed his eyes at his uncle, then George turned with a laugh and weaved through the corridors before bursting outside.

They ran through the courtyard, the rich scent of Spring in the air, avoiding grunting guards and gasping ladies, and then they were in the field. George, still ahead, ran through the ankle-deep grass, butterflies fluttering away, when suddenly the boy sneezed, slowing his pace, and Henry seized his moment.

He reached around George and grabbed his book, "It's mine!" and ripped it out of his sweaty hands just as Hal tackled George to the ground.

The action had appeared aggressive but to Henry's relief the two older boys were laughing as they wrestled for a moment, then got up, panting through bursts of laughter.

George wiped his nose on his sleeve, breathed a laugh, "Take it," he said to Henry as Hal brushed his sweaty brown hair from his brow, "It was but the bait to get you to follow."

Henry tucked his book against his chest and frowned at George, "What is it you have in mind today? Riding? Hawking?"

George jerked his head to the side, then skipped into a jog. Henry, as always, followed. And Hal followed him.

It was a particularly warm day. A layer of gauzy cloud had trapped the heat and thickened the air. Sweat had gathered in Henry's armpits and down his back, but when their goal appeared in the distance he no longer cared.

Moments later, they had reached the archery grounds and Henry selected his bow and quiver as servants appeared as if out of nowhere and prepared the stationary target.

As soon as the servants had moved into the clear Henry had taken an arrow from his new leather quiver – a New Year's gift from his father worth twenty shillings! – and pulled his bow string tight.

"One shilling says you can't hit it dead centre," George goaded his nephew now as he whispered hot breath into Henry's ear.

He may be the youngest of the three, but Henry's aim was perfect, and as George spoke the words, a grin twitched at the corners of Henry's lips.

"Not that I need your shilling," the king's son said as he released the arrow and turned to George, knowing without looking that he had hit the target.

Hal, watching from the sidelines, gasped.

"Of course not," George teased, his black eyebrows raised, his smirk gone, "Not with your £4000 yearly income from the king just for being *you*."

"Two shillings says you cannot hit even the boss," Henry said, dishing the banter back at George.

George snatched the bow from Henry, "Give me that," and he trudged to take his place facing their target.

He positioned the bow and arrow and pulled the bowstring taut.

"Crooke is coming," Henry said suddenly then, as the three boys observed the straw boss in the distance.

Hal looked back between the tutor and George.

But George did not react, one eye closed as he took his aim.

"George," Henry warned, his eyes flicking to their tutor as he stormed towards them, red-faced, "Crooke is right there."

"Hush, *princeling*," George muttered, then let loose of his arrow.

Henry's heart stopped to see his friend take the shot when their tutor was but three feet from the target, his aim not being reliable enough to have risked it. And he was ashamed to realise he had gasped in horror at George's recklessness.

"GEORGE BLOUNT!" Crooke's scolding voice called out then, and though his face was bright with anger, Henry breathed a sigh of relief to see he was not hit.

"You owe me two shillings," George sneered at him over his shoulder.

And sure enough, the arrow was embedded in its intended object, *just* on the outer line.

"You get BACK to your lessons, right this instant!" Crooke exclaimed, pointing his finger at the ground before him as though he would summon them like dogs.

Henry thought he came *this close* to stomping his foot at them. George shrugged and shoved Henry's bow against his chest.

"Your call," George said, and Henry looked from his raging tutor to his unbothered friend.

"You stay, if you like," Henry said after a moment's thought, "But I should like to exercise my mind for the remainder of the day."

And he tried to ignore George's mocking scoff as he walked back inside, Hal falling in step beside him.

While Henry enjoyed physical activities far more than taking part in lessons, he believed that to be a well-rounded individual he must engage in all aspects of his learning, much to George's contempt.

But truth be told, he enjoyed writing to his mother and stepfather of the things he had learned that week, especially when he would receive letters from them in return telling him how proud they were and how much they missed him.

News came that his mother had had another strong baby boy, that the brother who was but a newborn when Henry had left was now a cheery and strapping toddler, causing havoc at every turn, and that his beloved sister Elizabeth still missed him so much that she cried herself to sleep some nights.

Henry's heart would pinch with sadness to hear such news, feeling, not for the first time, that he would rather be home with his family than to be stuck here with titles and pretend duties. But, as with each letter, he would fold it in half, sniff away his tears, and tuck it in his breast pocket for the day, before returning to what was expected of him. It was the least he could do, knowing his family would benefit from his advancement, even if it meant increasing the space and time between them.

Chapter 6

February 1527
Greenwich Palace, London

The rumours that had circulated some years earlier that the King of England intended to name his illegitimate son his heir was resurrected when the matter of the boy's marriage was broached.

"We must make use of what means we have at our disposal to interrupt this union between France and Italy," Wolsey said passionately to the council as he stood before them, documents in his hand and spittle flying from his lips.

Charles Brandon shrank back slightly to avoid the downpour, his mouth pinched in dislike of the man.

"The king and I have discussed the matter at length," Wolsey went on, nodding once at his king as he sat silently at the head of the council table, "And Lord Richmond would be a fine match for Catherine de Medici, an offer which will hopefully counter the interest in her by the French. And as niece to Pope Clement VII, it would be an excellent match for His Highness' only living son."

The members of the council nodded and mumbled in agreement, "The boy is a useful bargaining chip for marriage negotiations," Charles called as he looked to Henry, "a useful asset in the international marriage market."

"Indeed," Wolsey agreed at the same time that the king nodded his head, "Richmond may be illegitimate but as a recognized son of the king, as well as his recent grandeur, Italy would be knaves not to consider him."

"Logically, Richmond is a better prospect of marriage than the French King's second son," another council member said pensively, tugging at his beard, "Richmond being the *only* living son of the king is nearer the throne of England than Henri d' Orleans is as the second born of the King of France. Our boy may have been born out of wedlock, but if the queen produces no male heirs, Your Majesty need only legitimize him. It has been done before –"

"But it is not yet a route we wish to take, my good sir," the king interjected, smiling secretly to see his long-term plan taking shape in his councils' minds, as though it were their own idea, "Let's not revive old rumours. Today is but for marriage negotiations. And if the Medicis accept our offer, my son will be a wealthy man with connections to the Pope himself, as well as providing an alliance with Italy and thwarting a Franco-Italian union."

March 1527

Though Catherine de Medici was but six-years-old, her uncle, Pope Clement VII, jumped at the chance to betroth her to the highest bidder. And the highest bidder – with the most lucrative prospects – was France.

"It is not the only marriage prospect at our disposal, Your Highness," Wolsey reminded his king, hoping to settle his master's troubled mind, "Maria of Portugal is an even better match."

"Yes, but Portugal is not constantly threatening us as France is," King Henry replied, thinking of the oxymoron that was Francis I, for though Henry hated the man *and* his country, he also secretly admired him, "I had hoped my son would be enough to bait the pope away from France."

"It was greed that led the pope's decision, not worth," Wolsey replied, though he knew how pitiful the offer of Henry Fitzroy must have looked beside that of a Prince of France.

"Maria of Portugal is a true princess," Wolsey went on, "A much better match for your son than that Medici commoner."
Henry chuckled lightly at that, a breath of joy escaping him to hear the jibe.

"True," he said, "Let's see if this match sticks, Wolsey. Having my son betrothed to a legitimate *infanta* would do wonders for his worth in the eyes of the people."

May 1527
Sheriff Hutton Castle, Yorkshire

"Have you heard the gossip?" George whispered to Henry one morning as their tutor turned his back on them to riffle through a pile of books on his desk. The old man was muttering absentmindedly under his breath.
Henry cast a glance to Crooke, then to George, "What gossip?"
George licked his lips excitedly, "I hear things at court are not smooth sailing. The king has taken a new mistress…"
At the news, Hal's dark gaze fell briefly on George.
"Ah!" Crooke called then, before turning to face them, holding a book aloft, "Here it is."
Henry flashed George a look that said they would speak later, though he could not begin to fathom why on Earth it mattered that his father had turned his attention to some other woman.

King Henry VIII had grown tired of his mistress Mary Boleyn some time ago and discarded her, before directing his focus to her younger sister the previous year – and the king's audacity had not gone unnoticed.
The court's chatter had not rested long upon the king's behaviour, however, for another, much more interesting development had become the centre of everyone's attention: this new love interest of his did not appear to *want* their handsome king's consideration.
As the previous mistress' sister, the lady had seen, first-hand, the shame an affair with the king could bring upon a woman. Because when the king ultimately tired of her, that lady's name would be sullied throughout England, and Anne Boleyn had had no intention of giving herself to a man that was not her husband.

She would not become the second Boleyn girl whose reputation the king would ruin.

However, he was the king. And one could not simply say 'no' to the King of England. And so, when his lingering gazes from across the room had turned into poems sent to her in secret, suggesting his interest in her to be becoming more intense, Anne had decided that some distance would best be put between them. And she had left the court for the sanctuary of her family home, Hever Castle. Surely, with her out of sight, he would turn his attention to another lady within the week.

But no matter the distance or the amount of time Anne had put between them, it seemed the king would not be deterred, and he had persisted in his pursuit of her by sending her letters and gifts, begging her to return to court.

He is in love with you, Anne's younger brother, George, had teased her one morning over breakfast when yet another messenger had arrived, this time bearing a gift of a sapphire necklace and a note from the king.

Anne had ignored her brother and the necklace and peeled open the note.

Read it aloud, George had said, laughing easily and seeing nothing wrong with the receiving of grand gifts, as the Boleyn family had done during their sister, Mary's, affair with the king.

Anne had not replied, scanning the letter quickly before tossing it into the fire.

Anne! George had exclaimed, his playful tone gone, *What did it say?*

Anne frowned, *It does not matter*, she had said.

But it had mattered.

For within that letter, the king had proclaimed his undying love for her and declared that he wished for her to become his royal mistress – something Anne had been fearing for some time when his letters had evolved from whimsical to passionate.

Send the necklace back, she'd told the messenger, who had frowned in confusion, unsure as to whether he had understood correctly.

Anne, George had called from behind her, *What the Devil are you doing?!*

Send it back, Anne had repeated, ignoring her brother, *Tell His Highness I must decline his offer.*

But – much to Anne's distaste – the king had not given up on his quest for her.

And eventually, she ran out of gentle rejections.

June 1527
Greenwich Palace, London

"I will have her, Charles," the king told his closest friend one evening after yet another of the many gifts he'd sent Anne Boleyn at Hever Castle had been returned, "I will have her, if it is the last thing I do."

"She is toying with your affections, my king," Charles told him, hoping to steer Henry away from his obsessive pursuit. For, after months of polite and repeated rejections, it was clear enough – to Charles Brandon and most of the court at least – that Anne Boleyn did not care for the king's interest.

But her rebuttal only spurred him on in his pursuit, as though this were but a clever game, a chance to woo and court the lady as a chivalric knight.

"It is not the girl you desire," Charles advised again, "But the chase! This cat and mouse game will lead to ruin. She's playing you for a fool!"

The king fixed his hard gaze on his friend then, "She does not *play* me," he said gruffly, refusing to see what was right in front of him, "She is but more virtuous than those who came before her! All the others who gave themselves to me easily were nothing but *whores*, eagerly sucking at the teat of the crown, willingly bedding me for what grandeur I might bestow upon them and their families – but not she! No. This angel is different, Charles. You do not understand! She does not care for my jewels or for my status. She wants only me."

Charles shook his head and sighed deeply, "But you are not just a simple man. If she truly wished to have you, she would do so in any way she can. And that is as your mistress."

"Not so…" the king added casually, shrugging one shoulder. Charles frowned deeply and watched as his friend plucked an apple from the bowl on the table and took a bite. He chewed slowly as he stood with his back to the fire, casting his face in shadow.

"Whatever do you mean, Henry?" Charles asked.

Henry swallowed and examined his apple then as if it were the most interesting thing in the world.

"Mistress Anne made a curious proposal," he said, a smirk twitching upon his thin lips, "An offer I would be unwise to dismiss."

Charles licked his dry lips, impatiently waiting for his king to stop speaking in riddles.

"Anne loves me, Charles," Henry said then, "She has not said so, but I can sense it in the way she shivers when I am near."

Charles did not dare to point out that fear or nervousness – even annoyance – could lead to the same reaction.

Henry continued, "She may continue to reject my gifts, may continue to tell me that 'no, she does not want me'. But she has quite clearly told me otherwise when she gave me an ultimatum."

"What ultimatum, Henry?" Charles croaked, disturbed to see the king so blinded by his passion, and his inability to accept defeat.

The king took another bite of his apple and chewed before tossing it, half uneaten, into the fire, sparks flying up into the hearth, "It was quite simple really: she made it perfectly clear that she would only ever lay with whomever claimed her as his wife."

Failing to see where the lady had made her supposed ultimatum, Charles screwed up his face, "How is that –?"

"A wife, Charles," Henry interrupted, grinning with glee, "That is what she wishes for me to make her. Not my mistress, not my whore. Don't you see? The ultimatum: If I *want* her, I will have to *marry* her."

Except, King Henry was already married...and in order to achieve his new goal, he would have to rid himself of his lawful wife.

"As far as I'm concerned, our marriage is at an end, Katherine," King Henry informed his wife of eighteen years one evening.

The queen's chest jerked as if he had punched her.

Though they had not lain together for many moons, and he had betrayed her more often than she could count, she had not expected this.

When there had been a knock at the door and her regal husband had entered her private chambers for the first time that year and dismissed her ladies, Katherine had allowed herself to believe that he had seen reason. That he had come to his senses and was returning to their marriage. Maybe even that he had missed her.

How wrong she had been.

"We continue without a male heir," he said monotonously now, as though he'd practiced this little speech in the mirror, "And you and I both know that a king needs sons for the wellbeing of his kingdom. I wish for this marriage to cease."

Katherine could do nothing but stare at the man before her, her mouth hanging slightly open in shock and her eyes blinking quickly in confusion.

"To cease?" she managed to mumble, puzzled.

"You and I were never legally married," he stated hotly, "Your marriage to my brother forbade it."

"My marriage to Arthur remained unconsummated, as you well know, husband."

Henry straightened his back but did not answer, giving Katherine a glimpse of the truth.

Did he think she did not know him well enough to catch his mannerisms? After nearly two decades of marriage and three decades since their first meeting, when he had been just a young boy and she a frightened fifteen-year-old, Katherine knew this man perhaps better than he knew himself. She had watched him grow from a gangly nine-year-old to the athletic and handsome man that stood before her today. Had witnessed his development, even helped to shape it; and that one slight action of his told her more than he had hoped to convey.

"You don't really believe what you are saying," she deduced, "You cannot possibly. You know my marriage to your brother was not fulfilled, that I was a virgin when I married you. Our wedding night, the bloodied sheets. You saw the proof with your own eyes!"

Henry jerked up his chin, "You cannot fight it, Katherine," he argued, "I have written to the pope. I have asked him for an annulment under the grounds that you are my sister by law. You are Arthur's widow, and no queen of mine."

Though Katherine had seen his jaw tick at the brazen lie, it hurt her soul nonetheless to hear the words spoken aloud by the one she loved. And though she had accepted his contempt towards her over the years, she had never considered him capable of being this cruel.

"Henry –" she beseeched, taking a step towards him.

But he pulled back, as though scared of what he would do if she came too near – perhaps drag the truth out of him simply with her gentle touch.

"It is done, Katherine," he said, standing his ground, "I have no more use for you. Or our daughter."

It was the wrong thing to say, however, for to mention their only surviving child suddenly fuelled a fire within the Queen of England.

"Mary is innocent in this," she reminded him, "And you cannot think to toss her aside. She is your heir!"

At that, Henry's lips stretched into a slow smirk, "By the time I have achieved my goal, I shall have half a dozen heirs running around the court. Half a dozen *male* heirs, Katherine. Something *you* failed to give me!"

October 1527
Sheriff Hutton Castle, Yorkshire

"*Pssst!*" George's sharp voice caught eight-year-old Henry's attention as he and ten-year-old Hal were about to enter the classroom.
They turned to the sound and saw George's acne-pocked face peering around the corner.
"I'll pay you a handsome reward not to attend lessons today," George offered, the perspiration on his forehead shining in the sunlight that peeked through the window.
Henry looked at Hal, then to his destined course, then back to George. His blue eyes narrowed briefly in thought before hurrying away from his duties, his face moulding into a mischievous grin as the two boys sped off down the stairs, Hal just a tick behind.
"The day is too brilliant not to spend it outdoors," George explained as he led the way, stopping only once to bow coquettishly at a handful of maids as they crossed paths, two of which giggled inanely at his flirtation.
He was right, Henry thought as he glanced outside, the sun had re-emerged for the first time in three weeks, during which time thick, gloomy clouds had taken the sky hostage.
George burst out into the courtyard with an exaggerated inhale, his arms stretched out wide as though he would embrace the sunshine.
"Let's take the horses and race," he suggested.
Henry shrugged, always easy to go along with whatever his friend suggested, and followed as George took off running.
Once at the stables, the boys awaited their mounts, which would need to be brushed and saddled before their excursion, and as they waited, they sat on the grass behind the large shed, to avoid detection from their no doubt disgruntled tutor.

"I don't know how much longer Crooke can take this," Henry chuckled once they were seated and he risked a peak around the corner.

"The vein on his forehead is probably throbbing as we speak," Hal added, grinning mischievously.

George shrugged, forced out a silent burp, "What can he do?" The question was rhetorical, Henry knew, but before he could even look away, George gasped, remembering something.

"It looks like the new mistress is to be more, in time," he said. Henry and Hal looked at him, puzzled.

George raised his eyebrows at them, coaxing them to understand, "You know," he went on, "The Boleyn woman. The second one."

"What about her?" Henry asked, disinterested in the matter. He looked over his shoulder to gauge the arrival of their horses. Surely his father would tire of her soon too, he thought. It had been months since young Henry had first heard of her and the scandal that was her rejection of the king's gifts. From what the boy had heard, she had, since then, given in and been paraded through court as the king's new love.

"The king has proposed marriage," George said.

At that, Henry gave him his full attention. Hal, too, was sitting forward with a frown etched between his dark brows. He had not heard of this latest news, though the woman was his cousin.

"Marriage?" Henry repeated, "But how? My father is already married."

George picked at the grass beside him, barked a short, sharp laugh, "It's the talk of the country," he said, as though Henry was a fool not to know already, "King Henry claims his marriage to the queen is not a true one, that this Anne Boleyn will grant him the sons he deserves."

Henry flinched at George's words, but the older boy did not even notice. Or maybe he didn't care.

Hal flashed a glance at Henry.

"It will make you so much less important once the king has sons that he can actually give the throne to," George said, and Hal sat back on his haunches, stunned by George's candour.

Henry swallowed hard, raised his chin, "I don't even want the throne," he said, realising for the first time that he had, subconsciously, long believed it would one day fall to him by default.

After all, he was the king's only surviving male child.

But for how long...?

George sneered, breathed a disbelieving laugh, "Sure," he said quietly, "As if you've never thought about it."

Henry tensed with anger to hear his tone, to hear the news, to hear the voice in his head telling him he would lose what should be his by right, though he had never before realised he'd even wanted it.

"How do you know all this, anyway?" Henry said then, standing up in his frustration, "How do you always *know?* You seem to pick up gossip like hems gather mud!"

George stood up slowly, brushed his slacks down with his dirty hands.

Counterproductive, Henry thought in disdain, suddenly seeing his uncle in a different light.

George was towering over Henry now, as he always did, being that he was five years older. But for the first time, it felt menacing, and the younger boy took a step back, looked to Hal for reassurance.

Strength in numbers.

"It serves me well being kind to those who run your household," George said slowly, "The cooks, the servants. They all have stories to share. Stories from court, stories of their lives."

He moved around Henry and Hal then as though he walked on some moral high ground, "You may find that those *beneath* you have a lot to say. Maybe if you hadn't been blinded by your sudden elevation, your glittering new status, you, too, could be as in the know as us *small folk*."

And Henry watched his friend – was he even his friend? He certainly appeared to have a lot of contempt for him – walk away, calling into the stables that his horse need not be prepared after all.

Greenwich Palace, London

Despite the king's plan to acquire a new wife to give him legitimate male heirs, he would not forget the son he had already sired.
Henry Fitzroy, though rarely in the king's line of sight, was always on his mind and exceptionally dear to him; and he felt a burst of joy whenever Cardinal Thomas Wolsey would bring word from Yorkshire of the boy's advancement.

"Richard Crooke continues most pleased with Lord Richmond, Your Grace," Wolsey told him one afternoon as he and the king headed to the great hall for a banquet.

"He is supremely skilled at translating and has a keen interest in Greek. However," Wolsey inhaled to suggest his annoyance, "Crooke does inform me that his classmate, George Blount, is a nuisance."

Henry frowned as they turned a corner and a handful of ladies curtsied as they strode past, "How so?" the king asked, not even granting them a quick scan, for no other woman mattered to him now that he had set his sights on Anne Boleyn.

"Crooke claims the older boy – his maternal uncle, as you may recall – is most disagreeable, often insulting Crooke and undermining his authority. So much so that oftentimes Richmond partakes in the disrespecting of him as his tutor."

King Henry shook his head slowly, taking it all in.

"There is more," Wolsey continued, looking ahead briefly and seeing the king's throne at the end of the great hall, the long tables set up for a feast and the many courtiers drinking and laughing, "Blount is no doubt a bad influence on your son, Your Highness. And Crooke has recommended he be removed from Richmond's household, since he is encouraging

Richmond to forsake his studies for...more entertaining pursuits: horse riding and archery and so forth."

Henry walked ahead then to take his seat on his gold throne, to oversee the entrance of all the nobles before the celebrations began. Then he looked his advisor up and down, waiting for the punchline.

When it didn't come, Henry exclaimed, "Oh! You are serious?"

Wolsey flinched, tucking his hands in the opposite sleeves of his red robe, "Indeed, my liege."

The king laughed then, a guffaw that echoed through the hall and which caused several courtiers to look their way.

"Wolsey, my good man," the king said between breaths, "Let the boy pursue the great outdoors! Riding. Archery. Those *are* a man's sport."

"But, my king," Wolsey countered, "He is your son. And as your son, Richmond is in need of a certain education."

Henry waved his hand before him, "Let him get on with it, Wolsey. If anything, it only strengthens my pride for him. If he prefers to hunt, hawk and ride, let him do just that! After all, he *is* my son."

Wolsey exhaled slowly through his nose, tried again, "Perhaps a new tutor would be the best course of action. One that the Blount boy has not stripped of authority with his disrespect."

Henry waved his hand, "Very well, Wolsey," he said, bored of the subject, "Whatever you believe to be best."

And the Cardinal couldn't help but feel uneasy that the king no longer seemed to heed his wisdom as readily he once used to.

Chapter 7

May 1528
Greenwich Palace, London

It was now common knowledge throughout England that the king intended to – somehow – marry the Mistress Anne Boleyn.
Despite her initial attempts to gently renege his propositions, Anne had evidently given in, whether due to her family's persistence that she ought not to look a gift horse in the mouth or her own change of heart, however, no one but she knew.
Nevertheless, it appeared to be love. At least on Henry VIII's part.
He sent her endless love letters comprised of romantic odes and promises of bliss. He even gifted her a buck that he had hunted himself – which was a splendid gift of status, since the king owned a significant portion of England's forests, and it was otherwise illegal to kill his deer. This in and of itself suggested to the whole court and country that Anne Boleyn meant a great deal to the king. He bestowed lands and titles upon the Boleyn family, rising them higher than they had ever dreamed possible. She was with him at all times, often *instead* of the queen herself, which was not always well received by the nobles and the people. Many deemed his efforts to replace the regal Katherine of Aragon with his mistress as a grotesque undertaking. But Henry did not care, for he was completely blinded by his obsession.
Henry VIII was a man who desired nothing more than to be remembered.
And now, after twenty years on the throne of England, Henry VIII was yet to achieve either glory *or* male heirs.
But he held onto the belief that surely, any day now, he would receive word from Pope Clement VII that his request of an annulment would be granted. And when that glorious day

came, he would waste no time in marrying his new love, who would undoubtedly grant him many sons.

But until then, Henry would turn his mind to the other means at his disposal in the hope of securing his succession. Namely, by making use of the son – and daughter – he already had.

"You wish to marry your son…to your daughter?" Thomas More asked his king after he'd shared the idea with his most trusted councillors.

The proposal of marriage of Henry Fitzroy to the *infanta* Maria of Portugal had not been successful, and instead of moping, King Henry had had this opportune epiphany.

"Your illegitimate son," Charles Brandon mulled, hoping to clarify his confusion, "To your legitimate daughter?"

The king clenched his jaw, not even gracing them with a nod of his head. They had heard what he'd said. They had understood it. Let them come to terms with it by themselves.

"I think it is an excellent idea," Wolsey chimed in.

"Of course you do," Charles retorted, "Anything the king says is accepted by you. Do you even *have* a thought of your own?"

Wolsey merely side-eyed the younger man, raising his chin that little bit higher.

Thomas Wolsey was between a rock and a hard place. As the king's right-hand man, he had been appointed with the task of seeking an annulment from the queen. A task which was appearing more and more impossible to complete when Wolsey's *other* master – the pope – did not wish to grant it. But Wolsey had decided to continue fighting on behalf of his king, choosing his Earthly gratifications over the preservation of his immortal soul. And he only hoped he had chosen wisely.

"It is not *unheard of*," More said then as he thought, "It would end your search for a male heir. If your daughter would continue as your successor and Fitzroy, as her husband, would be her king consort. It would continue the Tudor line."

Henry waved his hand in the air then, "Logistics may be discussed in the years to come."

More nodded, looking his king in the eye, "I am not totally opposed to it," he said carefully, "I am sure, with time, we shall all see it as you, sire."

"You will need a rock-solid dispensation from the pope," Charles Brandon informed him, his thick eyebrows bunched together in distaste for the idea, "As half-siblings, he will need to grant his papal authority."

"I have no doubt I shall receive it," the king said with a smug sigh, "As well as word about my annulment to my marriage to Katherine at any moment."

More and Charles shared a quick, sceptical look.

After months of waiting for an answer, they were not so sure of that.

"The irony of it must be broached, however, Your Highness," Thomas More said then, his dislike of the king's pursuit to separate from his legal wife having been a topic of heated discussion between the two since he had first thought of it.

More was a devout Catholic who believed in the pope's divine ruling, and was loyal to the rightful Queen of England. He was the king's man through and through, faithful to him and his court; but that being said, More would not turn his back on what he believed to be right. And in this case, Henry VIII's wish to annul his marriage to the queen was not only blasphemous, it was also political suicide. Katherine was the daughter of Spain, nephew to the Holy Roman Emperor, and beloved by the realm. To seek to replace her with another so disgracefully would – and already was – cause great public unrest.

"The irony, Thomas?" Henry asked, narrowing his ice-blue eyes at him.

Thomas More cleared his throat, not in unease, but in the hope of making himself perfectly clear.

"It will be a topic of conversation all around the kingdom, Harry," More explained, "And you cannot believe that not a single man or woman will see the blatant hypocrisy of it? As I said, I am not opposed to the idea – as incestuous as it may be, if the pope allows it and you so wish it, so be it – but you cannot think the people would accept your double standards."

Henry, failing – or unwilling – to understand, looked from More to Charles to Wolsey, the latter two averting their gaze.

"Come now, Harry," More continued with a low chuckle, the only person in King Henry's close circle that still called him by the name of his youth, "You must see it. Surely you cannot think to sanctify a union between your son and your daughter – two half-siblings – but in the same breath demand an annulment for your marriage to Queen Katherine under the grounds that she is your 'sister-in-law'."

At that, Henry flinched. He had not noticed the parallels until then.

"Which is it, Harry?" More concluded, almost goading him to see reason, "You are either accepting of such close familial marriages, or, my king, you are not?"

Sheriff Hutton Castle, Yorkshire

"I hear you are to be betrothed," George's tone was mocking as he picked dirt out from underneath his fingernails.

By now, George was no longer a boy but a young man of fourteen, with a voice that hitched up and down involuntarily and oily skin on his forehead and nose.

They had worked past their differences, boys being very easily able to return to their previous level of friendship – superficial as it was – after a disagreement. But Henry was not too naïve to understand that their circumstances played a big role in their camaraderie.

"Did you hear who to?" Henry Fitzroy replied, eyeing his teenaged uncle suspiciously, then he leaned forward to pick up a handful of pebbles and began tossing them lazily into the fountain before them, the same one they liked to sit by ever since he hit that frog on the head. As it turned out, the frog hadn't been unconscious like they'd thought, the impact of the pebble having killed it instantly. Henry still shuddered to think of how they poked and wriggled its dead body about for hours afterwards, thinking it merely knocked out.

George cocked his head to one side then and looked down at the dirt between them as he drew random squiggles with a stick, "A few apparently," he said, ever the detailed storyteller.

Henry rolled his eyes and was about to stand up when George spoke again.

"One was some rich commoner from Italy. I don't remember her name. Something difficult to pronounce, even without a *lithhhp*," he said the word mockingly, the same way Henry would have done when he was six, before his adult teeth had grown in and before he'd learned to control his speech impediment.

Henry flashed a quick look to Hal who sat beside him, embarrassed that he should hear of his childhood shortcomings. But Hal's expression was blank. Unlike George, there was no judgement from him.

In the past, Henry would have dished banter right back at George, but since their discord, the air between them had changed. George's remarks no longer appeared as harmless jesting.

George flashed Henry a smirk when the younger boy did not react. He'd gotten good at that lately, not reacting. For though he was King Henry's son, he had inherited his mother's patience.

"Probably best you didn't marry her," George continued, "Imagine it –"

"So not her then," Henry interrupted, standing his ground against the older boy's disparagement, "Who else?"

George chuckled, wiped his sleeve across his greasy cheek, "One was a princess of Portugal I believe," he continued, "But I hear she was swapped out for another princess."

He was grinning widely now, like a cat who'd caught a juicy, fat pigeon, "It's your sister," he finally said.

Henry frowned, "My sister? Elizabeth?"

George squinted his eyes at Henry as though he were stupid, "What good would that bring? And *gross*!"

"You said his sister," Hal backed Henry up.

George shook his head, "Not his sister Elizabeth, you dolts!" and he laughed, "The other one. The child of the king that actually has a chance of sitting on the throne. You know, his only *legitimate* child?"

Henry finally understood, and his face crumpled into shocked understanding while George continued to laugh.

"Are you certain?" Henry asked, his face paling at the news, and George nodded through his amusement.

He couldn't help it, but Henry's nose crinkled with displeasure. Granted, it wasn't as bad as he had initially thought when he'd assumed his full sister Elizabeth was to be his bride. But Mary was still his half-sister. And to imagine marrying her…well, at least he and George could agree on that: *gross!*

.

Chapter 8

October 1528
Greenwich Palace, London

Pope Clement VII sent his papal legate, Cardinal Campeggio, to England in order to hear the case which would determine the fate of the marriage between Henry VIII and Katherine of Aragon.

I have much hope for this, Wolsey, Henry had grinned at his advisor the night before Campeggio's arrival, practically holding the older man aloft by his lapels with excitement, *Campeggio will hear my case and do what is right.*

Wolsey had breathed a nervous chuckle, *I am sure you are right, Your Highness,* he'd said, silently praying it would be so, hoping that he had not chosen wrong by doing his king's bidding over of his God's. As a man of the cloth, it was a decision he had not made lightly. And he prayed every day that he would not be punished too greatly for it in the afterlife.

Campeggio, however, had been instructed by the pope that he was to procrastinate as much as he could in regard to the matter. He wasn't to make any decisions about the annulment, merely to listen and, more importantly, to stall.

With this in mind, Campeggio attended many discussions on the unique situation throughout the week that followed his arrival, and remained outwardly neutral, though he and his master were of course in the agreement that the marriage between Henry VIII and Katherine of Aragon was legal, regardless of King Henry's foot stomping.

But then, by the end of October, realising the king would not so easily relinquish his quest, Campeggio came up with an idea which he thought may very well be the solution to everything, and he sought permission from the pope before bringing it to the queen's attention.

"A nunnery?!" Queen Katherine exclaimed in disgust some days later, when the cardinal received word from Pope Clement VII that he may suggest it to her.

The cardinal couldn't help but flinch at her outburst. He had believed it to be a marvellous idea to resolve the issue for everyone. But it would seem the queen would not be deterred from hers and her daughter's rightful claims.

"Your nephew the Holy Roman Emperor King Charles V would not be offended by this outcome, he has assured me," Campeggio added, hoping to sway the queen.

Katherine breathed a laugh, "Forgive my bluntness but *I* would be! This will not do. Hear me when I say this: I intend to live and die in the state of matrimony in which God put me!"

It was not the reaction Campeggio had expected, for he had hoped that his suggestion would deter King Henry from continuing down this dangerous path of pursuing an annulment without the pope's consent.

And upon writing of the developments at the English court, as well as of his concerns, to his master, Campeggio received instructions to pursue a new tactic.

November 1528

"Cardinal Campeggio," the sentinel outside the king's chambers announced with a knock as the old man approached to meet with Henry VIII one evening.

The sound of shuffling paperwork could be heard, then shadows moved beneath the door's sill before the king accepted his company.

"Enter," he called, and Campeggio smiled wanly to hear the hint of disdain that lingered within the king. He had no doubt hoped the cardinal would arrive and immediately vote in his favour for his annulment. Campeggio did not do the king's work, however, but God's.

The guard opened the door, and Campeggio stepped inside, his red robes dragging along the floor as they always did at this time of night, when the hunch of his back was more prominent after a long, arduous day. Of which there had been many since his arrival in England.

"Cardinal!" the king called, feigning glee to receive him, "Come sit by the fire."

A servant appeared from the shadows and poured two glasses of wine, then disappeared from whence he came.

Campeggio sat down heavily, "Ah!" and gratefully brought the wine to his lips.

"Have you spoken to my wif – to Katherine?" Henry asked, clearing his throat, a darkness crossing over his face to have misspoken before the papal legate.

Campeggio nodded sombrely.

"The queen will not be made to enter a nunnery."

"Argh!" Henry exclaimed, raking his hand through his coppery hair, "I knew it. She is too stubborn."

The cardinal ignored the king's remark, for he – as well as all of Europe – believed the lady to be very brave indeed, as well as completely within her rights. And that it was, in fact, the king who was being stubborn.

"The pope has an answer for your other matter, Your Highness," the old man continued, looking the king in the eye.

Henry exhaled gruffly and sat back in his chair.

"Do I want to hear this?" he retorted, "Will it not simply be another 'no'?"

Campeggio smiled thinly, licked his lips, "I think you will be pleased with the news I bring in this regard."

The king's auburn eyebrows shot up in anticipation.

"In the interest of the continuation and preservation of the Tudor bloodline, and the queen's rejection of the suggestion that she join a nunnery, Pope Clement has granted you a positive answer in the matter of your son and your daughter."

Henry's mouth fell slightly open, his eyes shining by the flickering firelight, "The Pope grants permission for Princess Mary and Lord Richmond to marry?"

Campeggio nodded his old head slowly, "He does, indeed."

The king laughed, clapped his hands together once, so sharply the old cardinal winced.

"Well, this is *fantastic* news – !"

"There is...one condition the pope requires from you, however, Your Highness," Cardinal Campeggio interrupted, hoping to make his point while the king was on a high from the good news.

Henry sat forward in his chair, rested his elbows on his knees like an excited child, "Name it. Whatever the pope needs from me, I will do it."

Campeggio swallowed, conscious that the future of England, and perhaps even the future of Europe, hung in the balance.

Sheriff Hutton Castle, Yorkshire

"If the betrothal to the princess goes ahead," Henry's new tutor, George Fulbery, was explaining to them, "you would not marry until your fifteenth year. And even then, you would not be expected to consummate the marriage until you were both ready."

Henry, at nine-years-old, cared little for the topic of consummation, especially when it was to his *sister*.

Half-sister, he reminded himself. But it still turned his stomach to think of it.

"It is not uncommon to marry within the family," Fulbery continued, turning the subject into a lesson, "it is a practice that has been made use of since the dawn of time! To keep the bloodline pure or, in this case, to safeguard the Tudor dynasty. Why, the Holy Roman Emperor Charles V himself married his first cousin in 1526, and –"

"Cleopatra," Henry added, remembering the fact from his studies, "she married her brother to maintain the purity of their line, and they ruled Egypt together."

Fulbery nodded, impressed, "Indeed, my lord. So, you see it is not unheard of."

"Doesn't make it any less gag-inducing," George muttered beside Henry, pretending to vomit. To Henry's horror, he heard Hal sniggering behind him.

Henry swallowed his response, because – though he agreed – he was willing himself to accept it.

The idea of it alone would keep him up at night, his face scrunched up in thought as he imagined himself *kissing* his half-sister. Granted, he could hardly remember her, for they hadn't seen each other since last year's Christmastide. And even then, Henry had only caught a glimpse of her once as she and her ladies had entered at a banquet. They hadn't spoken in years. In fact, Henry could not remember the last time they had shared words beyond pleasantries. She was as much a stranger to him than any of the other girls his father had tried to betroth him to. And though they shared the same father, she was no more his sister than any other girl. Sure, they had the same blood running through their veins, but he felt no kinly affection towards the Princess Mary.

If he thought about it – which he often did – in the long run, it would not be all that bad.

If it had been a practice for centuries, and the Holy Roman Emperor himself deemed the act to be acceptable, then who was Henry to say it was not?

Henry had faced it: he was a nobody. A mere illegitimate son of the king. Sure, he had been bestowed with many titles and honours throughout the years; but as he'd gotten older, Henry had learned that there were titles his father was *not* granting him. Titles normally awarded only to the Heir Apparent: Duke of Cornwall, Prince of Wales.

Those were titles for the future King of England. And Henry thought that, if he were to marry the king's legitimate daughter…perhaps then *he* would be the one to receive them.

He would be someone then. Someone worthy of the throne of England itself – something which he had, over the years, grown to believe was surely his by right, as the only surviving son of the King of England.

Legitimacy be damned! The crown should go to him! The rightful Queen of England was past her childbearing years. And without another male child by her, the crown was certainly his for the taking!

A marriage to his half-sister would secure him that.

And for that honour, Henry had decided, it would be a small price to pay.

Greenwich Palace, London

"What will you do?" Charles Brandon finally asked his friend, broaching the condition Cardinal Campeggio had given the king, as the two men headed back to the castle after a morning of hunting, the other courtiers and guards tailing lazily behind.

The king had awoken with a splitting headache, one he knew would only be alleviated with exercise. And on a day like this, he wanted for nothing more than to kill something.

The boar they had tracked had given just the right amount of chase to get Henry's blood pumping, and the squeal it had emitted when the lethal arrow had pierced its neck had brought a grotesque grin to his face. He'd felt successful, thrilled, as they'd strapped the limp animal to their cart to bring it back to the palace for that evening's feast.

But upon their return, the proposition that loomed over him beset his mind, like dark clouds gathering before a heavy storm.

"It begs the question as to how much faith I have in Mistress Anne to grant me sons," Henry said slowly as he thought.

Charles nodded vaguely.

"To be allowed to pursue the marriage between Mary and Richmond, I am forced to relinquish my quest for Anne," Henry said, sighing heavily at the mention aloud of his conundrum, the condition the pope gave him if he wished for a dispensation to marry his two children to one another.

"But how can I?" the king asked under his breath then.

Charles dared not to reply.

"Through their union," the king continued, weighing up the pros and cons aloud, "I would be securing the Tudor bloodline. My son will be ten in the coming year, Mary thirteen. Even *if* I accept and they are betrothed, they cannot marry for another five years when the boy is of age."

Charles, suddenly fearful that the king would reject this rather perfect opportunity, cleared his throat, "But if you do decide to commit to your chase of Mistress Anne, you forfeit an immediate resolution to your matter of a successor. And the pope has not granted your annulment. You would not be able to marry the Mistress Anne and obtain legitimate heirs by her until after the queen – Until you are free to marry again…What if you have to wait *years?* What if, by then, Anne, like Queen Katherine, is not able to give you sons?"

Henry barked a laugh at that, "Come now, Charles. You know it is Katherine's fault I am even in this predicament. Any other lady I choose will indisputably be able to produce male children."

"But Anne Boleyn is not a young woman herself," Charles added swiftly, "In just a few years she will be the same age Katherine was when you gave up procreating with her."

The king looked at his friend with heavily hooded eyes, as though to warn Charles that he was pushing his luck.

Charles shook his head as they continued to ride, baffled by his friend's persistence.

If all this was *truly* about the stability for the country, he thought, then the king would accept defeat and settle for the marriage of Henry Fitzroy and the Princess Mary.

But Charles already knew the truth. This whole debacle was not about the wellbeing of the country and the preservation of the future. This was about Henry VIII getting what he wanted. And what he wanted most was Anne Boleyn.

The king's friend exhaled out of his mouth then, exhausted by the king's 'Great Matter' and his obsession with the woman, all because she would not give herself to him like all the others.

He looked over at Henry, riding majestically on his great steed, his back straight and only one hand holding the reins.

To Charles' disappointment, Henry no longer appeared at a loss, the frown that had been etched deeply between his brows since the pope's proposal had smoothed out.

He'd made up his mind.

And Charles scolded himself for having failed to steer Henry in the right direction.

December 1528
Sheriff Hutton Castle, Yorkshire

To Henry Fitzroy's great disappointment, his father the king had decided to renege the pope's offer of allowing the betrothal between him and his half-sister the Princess Mary to go ahead in exchange for the maintaining of the king's lawful marriage to Katherine of Aragon.

King Henry chose to continue pursuing his mistress instead, throwing away his twenty plus year marriage, as well as the strong and healthy son he'd already sired and need only legitimise. All of it, thrown out for a woman the king had not yet even bedded, a woman who he hoped would grant him a *real* son.

Young Henry's uncle George wiped imaginary sweat from his brow in relief of the news, then clapped Henry on the back.

"A lucky escape," he said with a grin.

But Henry did not return George's enthusiasm, too irked was he by the outcome. For by now, he had accustomed himself to the idea.

"Lucky," he repeated, angry for losing something that had never been his to begin with.

But it *almost* had been.

Henry had been *so close*.

And there was only one person to blame for his great loss.

Chapter 9

August 1529

Henry Fitzroy's time in the north was at an end after being summoned by his father to attend Parliament.
He and his household of two-hundred and forty-five servants including grooms, ushers, cooks, stablemen and chaplains made their way back to London, leaving the Council of the North to be run without its President.
It wouldn't make much of a difference, Henry thought, since it had only ever been a titular position, one where his presence meant more than anything he ever had to say. Not that he had ever said much of anything during the meetings, where everyone spoke for him. The council would manage just fine without him.
Besides, Henry was looking forward to returning, his new position as a member of Parliament meaning he would become part of the royal court. And since his stepfather, Gilbert Tailboys, had been created Gentleman of the Chamber two years prior in 1527, it meant that Henry would finally be reunited with his family. And he couldn't wait.
He was excited to meet his youngest brother, to show off his new skills, and teach his sister Elizabeth how to speak French. But above even all that, Henry yearned to distance himself from his uncle George Blount.
"Mother!" Henry called as soon as he spotted her beaming face among the crowd that welcomed him.
He swung from his gelding and hurried to her as she walked towards him with open arms.
Mother and son embraced, Bessie tearing up to feel his once-tiny body so tall and stretched against hers. His head now reached her shoulder, and in that moment, she could hardly remember where it had reached the last time they had held each other. She closed her eyes and breathed in his scent,

immediately saddened to note his child-aroma was replaced by one a little more acrid. Puberty was beginning to take hold of her little baby, and she hadn't even had the chance to watch his transformation from boy to man.

"How tall you've grown," she managed to say as they separated and she looked him up and down, "And so handsome!"

Henry looked down at their shoes with a lopsided smile, embarrassed.

His stepfather approached then, with a girl walking behind.

"Elizabeth?" Henry asked with an unsure smile, unable to connect the image of the gangly nine-year-old girl before him with the one he had in his mind of the chubby-cheeked four-year-old he remembered.

The girl smiled at him a little shyly, and he realised they had both changed. It would take some time to rekindle their relationship. Sporadic letters over the years had not been enough to maintain much of a bond.

"Come here, my boy!" Gil said now as he slapped Henry heartily on the back and pressed him to him briefly, "We're glad to have you back," he said, his deep voice filled with emotion, and Henry felt his chest quiver at the realisation that he, too, was very glad to be reunited with his family.

September 1529

Shortly upon his arrival in London, Henry – who was an Earl, a Duke, a Knight of the Garter, and former President of the Council of the North – was given another, brand new title.

"Lord Lieutenant of Ireland," he muttered to himself under his breath after the ceremony, testing it out on his tongue.

It was yet another noble status to add to his ever-growing list. But something was different about this honour, for in this occasion, he would also be granted a suite of rooms at Windsor that were usually reserved for the King of England's heir, the Prince of Wales.

"Not even the Princess Mary, who was Princess of Wales in all but official name, was given such grand suites," his stepfather informed him quietly, as the court was filtering into the great hall to celebrate the occasion with a banquet. Henry's red eyebrows shot up in wonder at the information, and he couldn't help but smile to think that his father was clearly – hopefully – grooming him to succeed him.

That fact did not go unnoticed by the rest of the courtiers, either, who Henry noticed were already gossiping behind their gloved hands.

Following the ceremony that saw Henry titled Lord Lieutenant of Ireland, the court settled in for a fine feast and a masque, which, judging by the raucous laughter and music that now filled the air, they were enjoying immensely.

Queen Katherine – like at most of his elevations throughout the years – was not present. On previous occasions it had been due to her dislike of his promotions, which she had made clear by choosing not to attend. But more recently, it had been because the king had forbidden her from joining, her replacement taking her position beside the king instead.

Henry had heard of these goings on for years, through second and third hand gossip that had travelled miles and likely been moulded and exaggerated. He had always thought that whatever rumours they heard in the north would have been blown out of proportion by the breaths of all those who had whispered them before they'd reached Henry's ears.

But now, as he sat among the court, enjoying the evening festivities, Henry noticed – as it could hardly be missed – how the Mistress Anne Boleyn was being paraded around by the king as though she were his wife already. Just as he had heard. The king even went so far as to seat her at the high table beside him, in the very place where the queen ought to sit. And Henry, even at just ten, thought it all rather tasteless.

Though he personally had no affiliation to the Queen of England, who had made her displeasure in his existence very clear, it all felt rather unpleasant in his stomach. Where was the loyalty?

As the food was served and the wine flowed, laughter filled the hall above the merry music. Noblemen were calling loudly to one another, their ladies tittering behind their hands or embroidered handkerchiefs, exchanging gossip and stories.

But there was no laugh greater than the king's, and young Henry would often turn his head towards the sound to find the cause of his happiness to be the Mistress Anne whispering in his ear or sharing a captivating tale with the table.

Henry watched the people at the high table, the king and Anne Boleyn at the centre, bookended by Charles Brandon and some ladies Henry only knew from sight. As he watched, their enjoyment became contagious, and a smile crept over the boy's face.

Mistress Anne must have felt his eyes upon them, for she suddenly looked towards him as she laughed.

She was pretty when she laughed, Henry noticed. But then her smile suddenly faded when their eyes met, and the boy was left feeling as though he'd been caught with his hand in the biscuit bowl.

He quickly looked away, turning to his stepfather who sat beside him.

"What irks the Mistress Boleyn so?" Henry asked him, as several lords and ladies rose from their seats to take to the dancefloor.

Gil looked up at the high table to catch the brief narrowing of eyes in their direction, before Anne Boleyn turned to smile back up at the king.

Gil chuckled quietly, "Other than Cardinal Campeggio and Wolsey failing to grant the king his annulment from the queen?" he asked rhetorically, then took a sip of his wine and spoke on, "Your success dampens hers," he said plainly, as if that were obvious.

Henry frowned, then looked up at the woman pretending to be the queen as she practically sat on his father's lap.

"How so?" he said, "From what I can see she is doing quite well for herself."

Gil turned away from the lovebirds and to his own wife who was dancing with Elizabeth in the middle on the crowd.

"Do not concern yourself with her," Gil said sagely, "The Mistress Anne is known for her temper. She will adore you one day and hate you the next. She is quite unpredictable."

"But why would she hate me at all?" the boy asked.

Gil shook his head, "Not *you* necessarily. She doesn't hate *you* whatsoever. It is what you represent that she does not enjoy. And tensions are growing here, my boy. She has much to worry about of late."

Henry frowned, then shook his head. He was still too young to easily comprehend adult reasonings. Politics, social statuses, what it all meant…He didn't think he'd ever understand.

"As the king's only son," Gil explained, sensing the boy's confusion, "she is in direct competition with you for the king's regard. If they do not wed and produce an heir soon, you continue his only living boy. And it is no doubt a concern of hers that the king will one day choose *you* over the potential of achieving a son by her. You and the Princess Mary are in direct competition with any future children she may give your father."

Henry scrunched up his face, unsure if he believed his stepfather's logic.

"But he chose *not* to elevate me," Henry argued, his eyebrows knitted together, "He has made his choice not to betroth me to my half-sister. He chose Anne."

Gil nodded as he looked out at the dancing courtiers, "Until they are wed, nothing is certain."

"Will you dance with me, husband?" Henry's mother now said as she stood smiling before them, interrupting their conversation. Then she looked to Henry with a pretty smile that he realised he had missed terribly, "Your sister wishes to play chess with you."

"Where is she?" Henry asked, craning his head to peruse the rooms.

Bessie nudged her chin over her shoulder, "Already at the games table. But I warn you, son. That girl has a keen eye for it. Do not underestimate her."

And then Bessie pulled her husband towards the dancefloor. Henry could hear his mother's laugh trilling as they disappeared into the crowd, and it warmed his heart. Their love gave Henry a glimpse of the kind of marriage he would one day hope to achieve.

He scanned the great hall again then, to find where his sister was setting up the chess pieces. He found her at the table nearest to the hearth in the west wing and nodded his head at her when their eyes met from across the room, to signify that he was on his way.

But before he started around the dancefloor, Henry glanced over at the king and Anne Boleyn, who continued busy whispering in each other's ears and feeding each other sugared grapes.

Gil's words suddenly made sense in the boy's mind, and a cold finger of understanding ran over his spine.

No, Henry thought as he walked away, *I must not underestimate her.*

Gil Tailboys may not have been born of great men, nor was he particularly well educated, but he was a man of quick wit and insight, and he understood *people* better than most.

Since 1517, when he began serving in Cardinal Wolsey's household, Gil had been carefully watching from the shadows while greater men did all the talking. He'd observed the king's reactions to both good and bad news, to losses, failures and the strenuous development of – sometimes brilliant – ideas. But as well as observing England's monarch, Gil had also kept an eye on those closest to him; and he had quickly learned that it was usually those that held the most secrets.

Which was exactly how Gil knew that the Mistress Boleyn was not as unperturbed as she was letting on.

The psychological and emotional strain all this must be taking on her aside, the return of the king's prodigal son had ruffled her feathers. And Gil, as a newly appointed Gentleman of the Chamber, was now in the prime position to know exactly *why*. King Henry VIII was becoming impatient…that much was clear. And an impatient king led to deviations from the plan.

"Until I have married Anne and fathered legitimate sons by her," the king explained aloud to his council one day following the boy's return, "I shall continue to work with what I have."
Charles Brandon, Thomas More and Thomas Wolsey nodded their heads in agreement.

"Your son's new title of Lord Lieutenant of Ireland shall open many doors for him," More said, a little too curtly for the king's liking.
Henry VIII knew his advisor and friend did not stand by him on his quest to replace Queen Katherine, so it was a pleasant change to hear his words of approval of Henry's other strategies. He only wished More would keep his disdainful tone in check.

"Yes," King Henry replied with the same tone as More, suggesting to him that his attitude was not going unnoticed, and Gil chuckled under his breath, observing the communication from the far wall where he stood.

"I myself was granted this honour when I was but three years of age!" King Henry continued, "And though Lord Lieutenant of Ireland is but another symbolic position, it represents my sovereign interest in the region and offers the possibility for more in the future."

"Exactly what 'more' did you have in mind, Henry?" Charles Brandon asked, moving slightly in his chair to escape the glare of the summer sun as it shone through the open window.
Gil leaned forward subconsciously, his interest piqued.

"We shall have to arrange for a wider education for my son if I wish to pursue this route," the king said, ignoring Charles' question, "I have thought it through. He shall head a council made up of the Archbishop of Durham as chancellor,

Bermingham as Chief Justice of the King's Bench, and John Rawson for his treasurer. They will all rule in his name, since my son is still just ten, but in time, he will be ready."

"Ready for what, Your Highness?" Charles tried again, and Gil noted that the rest of the council members were looking to one another with the same question in their eyes.

It seemed nobody but the king himself knew of this new idea. King Henry picked invisible lint from his sleeve, feigning innocence, "The boy is a replica of myself at that age, both in looks, knowledge and skill – *more* skilled in fact! At his age I was not as good a rider as he!"

Gil's chest burst with delight though Henry Fitzroy was neither his biological son nor had it been he who had taught the boy to ride. But pride to hear the boy be praised was there nonetheless, for it was but an extension of familial love.

But then the king continued, "In time, I expect to name my son ruler of Ireland."

The men froze, some looked back at their monarch with wide eyes.

"King of Ireland, in fact," Henry VIII persisted, grinning idly at his advisors.

Gil exhaled slowly at the grand announcement, his dark eyebrows risen high on his forehead to think that not Anne Boleyn, nor most of the court, would take this news well.

"Ruler of Ireland? Has the king gone mad?" Thomas More asked Charles Brandon rhetorically as they made their way to the tiltyard to observe the joust scheduled for that afternoon.

Charles did not reply, his expression being enough to show More that he was in agreement.

"Ireland will not accept this without a fight," More continued, "Not only does it show England's clear interest in control over the country but to assume they would be accepting of a bastard-born child to become their king…"

"It will lead to war, no doubt," Charles Brandon concluded, looking around to assess that his surroundings were safe from eavesdroppers.

More nodded his head, leaned in closer to Brandon as half a dozen courtiers passed them on the outskirts of the palace field.

"It would not unite England and Ireland either," More said as he contemplated the idea, "For Richmond is not the king's heir to the English throne. All it would lead to – if it would even be successful – is the creation of another, separate monarchy."

"Unless the king has not given up hope of proclaiming Fitzroy his heir after all," Charles deduced as they hovered near the entrance of the tiltyard.

They could hear commotion in the arena, people talking, laughing, cheering, while the horses were being prepared, and the jousters armoured.

"Do you believe that?" More asked, his voice hitching with uncertainty.

Charles shrugged, "Who knows what our king is planning these days," he said, "I myself cannot keep up with all his endeavours," and he made his way inside, concluding the conversation.

Thomas More watched him go, lost in his own thoughts for a moment.

"No, me neither," he mumbled.

The three equally shocking plans the king had put in motion in recent years flickering in More's mind then: the removal of the king's lawful wife in favour of a woman who has surely bewitched him, the naming of his bastard son as his successor of the English throne over his legitimate daughter, the creation of a new monarchy in Ireland which would have a future claim on the throne of England.

All those options would undoubtedly lead to disaster. All would lead to unrest, chaos and unnecessary deaths.

And no matter how much More considered each aspect, quite frankly, he could not decide which outcome would be the worst.

October 1529

Following his failure to secure an annulment, or to obtain the approval to wed his son to his daughter unless he gave up Anne, Henry VIII was most displeased; and it would be his former right-hand man, Thomas Wolsey, who would take the fall for these great disappointments.

"I release you from my service, Wolsey," King Henry said rather too casually one morning, at the beginning of their regular council meetings. Then he bellowed to the guards, "Get him out of my sight!"

Wolsey's eyes went wide at the order, "My king?!" he protested, disturbed to see his master turn on him when he – as a cardinal, a man of the cloth – had chosen to serve his king above his God, even when his conscience had spoken against it.

Henry did not look up from the paperwork before him, "You did not fight hard enough to obtain my goal."

Wolsey scoffed in disbelief as the guards hauled him from his seat.

"You cannot be serious, Your Highness," he whispered, fear and betrayal shining in his eyes and cracking his voice.

After everything he'd done, disregarding God in favour of his king's wishes, his outrageous *Great Matter*...and *this* is how he would repay him?

The guards were leading him toward the door, and his king would not even grace him with his attention. And Wolsey realised, much too late, that he had chosen wrong.

"My king!" Wolsey called, almost at the door, and when he understood that Henry would not forgive him, his face contorted in anger: "If I had served my God as diligently as I did my king, He would not have given me over in my grey hairs!"

At that, at last, the king looked up. But Wolsey saw only boredom in his gaze before the guards bundled him out the door. And he knew then, with the beauty of hindsight, that he had chosen wrong.

Chapter 10

December 1529

Due to Henry Fitzroy's age, his titles and positions were still very much in name only, just as they had always been, and though he was requested to return to London to become a member of Parliament in the House of Lords, he could not rightfully be expected to partake in the discussion and decision-making that would shape the country. Son of the king or not, he was still just a child.
His stepfather, Gilbert Tailboys, was called to take his place instead, being one of four members of Commons promoted to the Lords and being titled Baron Tailboys of Kyme with the honour.
And it was a privilege that Gil would carry to his grave.
"You look very handsome," Bessie told him on the morning of his first appearance in the House of Lords.
Gil grinned roguishly and pecked his wife on the cheek, "As long as you continue to think so when I am old and grey."
Bessie slapped him playfully on the arm, "Of course I shall," she said, pressing her body to his as they lingered by the door, savouring their time together before parting ways for the day.
She reached onto her tiptoes to kiss him in farewell when a *crash* and an exasperated groan was heard from the other room, followed by what sounded like a screech into a cushion.
They both looked in the sound's direction, Bessie sighing.

"Leave it with me," she muttered, already tearing herself away from her husband.
She heard Gil chuckle under his breath and turned towards him with a ready smile, but he was already out the door. Her smile faltered, and she inhaled deeply before turning back to her duties, pushing her pining to the back of her mind.
Truth be told, Bessie was feeling lonely.

Ever since their return to court, where they would now often attend jousts, dances, banquets, and were always around people, she had never felt quite so alone.

Her husband and sons' elevations were blessings – of course! There was no doubt about it. But with those grants came others, which, though she and Gil had been grateful, kept Bessie on edge.

Her and Gil's sons, George and Robert, were – by the magnanimity of the king – awarded the permission to be brought up as part of their half-brother's household, thereby receiving his noble education. It meant their futures would surely be secured.

But Bessie had been sceptical of the king's generosity, fearing that, after all these years, there was maybe more to King Henry's kindness than meets the eye. After all, he continued to this day to gift her jewels and bolts of exquisite cloth at New Year's celebrations. Something which no other of his mistresses was privy to.

There was nothing Bessie could do however, except to accept the wonderful offer of sending her boys to reside at court with her eldest son, as well as accept the gifts. And though she had been separated from all her sons now as they pursued a brighter future, it was the one child that had remained under her roof for which she was most concerned for.

"I hate Henry!" Bessie's only daughter, Elizabeth, hissed as her mother walked towards her now.

It was she who had caused the ruckus – which Bessie now saw had once been a vase – and she who had screeched into the cushion which now rested on her lap.

"I absolutely loathe him!"

Bessie reached for her daughter and cupped her pink cheek, choosing to scold her for the broken vase later, "You do not loathe your brother," she said.

"Why is it that he gets to study interesting things while I'm supposed to be content with sticking needles through handkerchiefs and sheets!"

The young girl flung herself back onto the lounger, her wavy strawberry-blond hair splayed out around her head like that of a mermaid's.

This outburst – like all the others in recent months – was not about her older brother's higher education, Bessie knew, but rather about what it represented.

Her daughter had grown up believing Gilbert Tailboys to be her father. It had been a natural development given the fact that the girl remembered no other paternal figure but he, and their close bond over the years had been quite evident. Gil had raised her as his own, had doted on her as such, too; which had been one of the reasons why Bessie had fallen so hard for him.

But in more recent months, Elizabeth had put two and two together.

She looked nothing like Gil. Nor did she bear any resemblance to her brothers Robert and George, who had both inherited Gil's dark hair and eyes. Elizabeth, like her brother Henry, had lighter features, hair the colour of the early morn and freckles splashed across her nose. Sure, their mother was fair-skinned and blond. But Henry's colouring matched that of his father, the king. And Elizabeth did not need a noble education to realise that if she and her older brother looked alike and he looked like his father, then she, too, must be the king's child.

Bessie had not denied it, when the girl had come to her and asked – for why would she? Bessie was not ashamed of her past, nor would she deny her husband's compassion in claiming Elizabeth as his when she was not. Such goodness should not be disregarded in the effort of saving face.

But all this new understanding of late had turned the young girl's stomach in knots, for not only did it burst her reality that the man she loved as a father was not, in fact, her father. But it also begged the question: why didn't her *real* father think her worthy enough to acknowledge as his.

She understood it – vaguely. She knew that being a girl *was* less favourable than being a boy.

But still it ached her heart to learn she had been discarded at birth due to her gender, before even being able to prove herself. And ever since this new knowledge, Elizabeth often found herself thinking of the Princess Mary, and how terribly sad she must be feeling throughout all this chaos – their father's 'Great Matter'.

For was it not only happening at all because she, too, had been born a girl?

But Mary, at least, was not a bastard, like Elizabeth was. And *still* their father did not think her sufficient to inherit the throne.

"Do you think my brother shall one day become the king's heir?" Elizabeth asked now, her tantrum having lost its wind.

The corner of Bessie's mouth twitched in thought, "Probably not," she said as she lay down beside her daughter and tucked her body against hers, like she used to when she was a baby, "Not now that the king chose not to marry Henry to the princess."

They were silent for a while, considering the outcome if only he had.

"I only wish also to be seen," Elizabeth said then, absentmindedly examining a strand of her hair.

"I know," her mother said, slotting her chin on Elizabeth's head, "But it is a man's world, Elizabeth. And in a world governed by men we shall never achieve their respect by throwing tantrums and pointing out the inequality of it all."

"But –"

"No 'buts', child," Bessie continued, her voice tender but firm, "You must accept the hand that you were dealt. Gilbert may not be your father by blood, but he is the father you all deserved. He has been a wonderful parent to all my children, including the two that are not his. That is a rare jewel to find."

Elizabeth turned to look at her mother, and Bessie tucked a strand of her copper hair behind her ear, "Be grateful, Elizabeth. The father you suddenly long for is no match for the one you already have."

Then Bessie wrapped her arms around her only daughter and sighed, a silence falling over them again.

And in that silence, with her mother's words curling around her, Elizabeth's young mind worked out an outrageous paradox: that while Gilbert Tailboys claimed her as his out of the goodness of his heart, her true father had not only dismissed her, but was now also actively dismissing a legitimate daughter in favour of a son he may never have.

Elizabeth being left unclaimed and nameless by the king aside; what he was doing to the daughter he had spent the last thirteen years nurturing was beyond shameful.

Gil Tailboys is a better man than King Henry, she realised.

And looking at it in this new light, Elizabeth had to wonder: when it came to fathers, at least, was she luckier than even the Princess of England herself?

April 1530

"I shall call it a night, my sweet," Gil told his wife early one evening, following a long and tiring day at court.

"Are you ailing?" Bessie asked, looking up from her needlework by the fire, Elizabeth following her gaze.

Gil shook his head, "No, Bessie. I am but tired. You girls enjoy the rest of your evening."

"Goodnight, Father," Elizabeth offered, smiling at him from across the room, her needle sticking out through the cloth, awaiting her regained focus.

Gil returned her smile, then, on second thought, walked back over to them and planted a peck on the crown of Elizabeth's head, "Goodnight, my daughter," then to his wife, "Goodnight, darling."

With a fatigued wave, he turned in for the night.

And to everyone's horror, he did not wake up the following morning.

*

As if to prove to Elizabeth that he had loved her as his daughter in life, Gilbert Tailboys had made arrangements for her in the event of his death. In his will, he left part of his Lincolnshire estates to be settled on Elizabeth, giving her an annual income of £200 a year.

He had done the same for his other two children, Robert and George, but failed to include his stepson, Henry Fitzroy. This was not done out of malice, for he had loved Henry as his own, but he had known that the boy would not ever want for anything as the acknowledged son of the king. And he'd had to primarily consider those who relied solely on him. Henry knew this, of course, and he did not begrudge his stepfather for even a moment.

Gilbert Tailboys, the recently appointed Baron and member of Parliament, was buried in Kyme Priory, leaving behind a wife and four children. They would all mourn him desperately.

But the politics of court never slowed even in the fog of grief, the diplomatic cogs continuing to whirr despite personal losses. For Bessie Blount being suddenly unmarried meant that a new opportunity was open for consideration.

Hampton Court Palace, London

Following Thomas Wolsey's fall from grace the previous year, Wolsey would attempt to regain his favour by gifting the king his impressive residence of Hampton Court Palace.

It had not always been a palace, Wolsey having spent vast amounts of money over the years to renovate what had once been a manor into a residence fit for a king.

Henry VIII accepted the gift, of course, but it did little to thaw the ice between them. And as soon as he was able, the king had moved his court there, marking it as his new favourite seat in all of England.

It was there that the already-aggravated king – who continued consumed with his need for an annulment – was given a proposition which would, yet again, make him question his faith in Anne Boleyn.

"They want me to consider Bessie Blount," King Henry confided in his closest friend, Charles Brandon.

He and the king were sharing a private moment by the pond yards in the King's Privy Garden. Henry had decided to take some time away from the hustle and bustle of the palace and to clear his mind with a spot of falconry, a sport he had enjoyed since childhood.

The two men observed the blue sky for a moment, a silence befalling them as they watched the gyrfalcon. Then Henry whistled, signalling the bird to return.

When Charles did not reply, Henry turned his gaze on him, "What are your thoughts on the matter?"

Charles raised his dark eyebrows and sighed. He knew of this proposition, for he had been among the council when it had been broached. He had not spoken on it then, however, and he was reluctant to do so now, no matter how much he believed it to be the perfect solution to the king's problems.

"Marrying your former mistress would end your quest for a son," Charles said deliberately, "and the pope would likely legitimise him. It has been done before, by John of Gaunt, as you well know."

Henry nodded slowly, "Of course. It is how I stand here today as King of England. His legitimised line is what led me to my fate."

Charles looked up at the sky again when he spotted movement in his peripheral vision. Henry followed his gaze.

In the distance, the two men laid eyes on the king's majestic falcon, then heard it call out to them. Henry raised his arm, donning a leather falconry glove that reached his elbow, in preparation for the bird's landing.

"Beautiful, isn't she?" the king asked rhetorically.

Charles nodded nonetheless, it was quite the incredible beast. The gyrfalcon drew closer, its large wings flapping and its great talons curled out before it, aiming for Henry's perched arm.

Upon landing, the king muttered lovingly at the feathered creature, stroking its head and back.

"You know the falcon," Henry said then, causing Charles to tear his eyes from the beautiful bird to his friend, "it symbolises 'one who does not rest until the goal is achieved.'"

Charles frowned, failing to understand.

"The falcon," Henry said again, "It is what Anne would choose for her emblem, she has said, when she is queen."

Charles cleared his throat, "Fitting," he replied, knowing it would be unwise to voice his true thoughts: that Anne Boleyn was reaching far too high and assuming far too much. She may never become queen, and yet she spoke and acted as though she already were, making too many enemies in the process. And Charles briefly thought of the time when she had not even wanted the king.

If only Henry had accepted defeat back then...

But of course, accepting defeat was not his strong suit.

Henry sighed audibly, irked by the situation he found himself in.

"If I were to take Bessie as my wife," Henry said, steering back to the issue at hand, "the pope may still not give me what I need."

Charles cocked his head to one side.

"He legitimised John of Gaunt's bastards," Henry explained, "that much is true: the Beauforts were legitimised. But they were barred from inheriting the throne."

Charles sucked air in through his teeth, he had forgotten this one crucial detail.

"Imagine, if you can, that I take Bessie instead of Anne, and Henry Lord Richmond is legitimised. Only for him to then not be able to inherit the throne after all."

"You would sire more sons by Bessie, no doubt, and those sons would indisputably be acceptable successors," Charles offered, "She is clearly fertile, having given Tailboys two strong male children during their marriage."

Henry nodded but Charles could already tell that his heart was not in it, "She is no longer a young woman," the king countered as he looked at the bird of prey perched on his arm and hooded it.

His friend stiffened, battling with himself as to whether he should give voice to his thoughts.

"The Mistress Anne and Bessie Blount are but a couple of years apart," he dared, "at least with Bessie you have literal proof of her fruitfulness."

Henry was silent for a long while, during which time Charles felt his hands beginning to sweat. Had he said enough? Or too much? Had he proven to Henry that his quest for the Boleyn girl may not end the way he had envisioned?

Charles had nothing personal against the woman, not *really*. Apart from the fact that her mere existence appeared to have bewitched the king in some way. But Henry's obsession with her was growing tiresome. And Charles was not the only one who thought so.

"I shall have to think on this issue further, Charles," the king said, "No matter what I decide, I must make haste with my annulment from Katherine. I have not given up. Thomas Cranmer has been dispatched to seek opinions of universities across Europe regarding the annulment."

Cranmer, Charles thought, *the man has been known to favour the new ways of thinking. His ambition for reform would once have been considered heresy...*

"Whether I marry Bessie or Anne," the king continued, "is as yet irrelevant while I continue shackled to Katherine."

Charles silently noted the hypocrisy of this entire situation, for not all that long ago, Henry himself had been titled Defender of the Faith by the pope following his public outrage at Martin Luther's reformist ideas; and now he was actively favouring men who would denounce the pope and the old ways. All so that he could rid himself of a wife that even the king knew was his by law.

Thinking he was about to be dismissed, Charles bowed his head and turned to leave, but then Henry spoke on.

"No woman can replace Katherine," he said, piquing Charles' interest for one mere moment, "not until she is either finally deemed as not ever having been my true wife..." the king paused, stroking the gyrfalcon tenderly and dashing Charles' hope, "or...until she is dead."

November 1530

Thomas Wolsey, who had spent his adult life rising higher and higher, climbing the ranks from a mere butcher's son to the second-most powerful man in all of England, died on his way to London to face his charges of high treason.

"I wanted him to pay for what he did!" King Henry bellowed, angry at his formerly favourite advisor for dying before he could be tried for treason.

"Surely death is payment enough," replied Thomas More, who had been appointed as Henry's new Lord Chancellor following Wolsey's removal from office.

Henry scoffed angrily, turning his back on More and staring into the flames in the hearth, "Katherine would say this was God's punishment," he mumbled after a moment, his blue eyes shining gold, "She would say it was a sign."

More inhaled, shifted in his seat, "Perhaps she would be right." Henry turned a disgruntled face to More, all but baring his teeth at his good friend, "Careful, Thomas," he growled, "I am well aware of your standing in all this. But do not presume to lecture me now. I was ready to execute the last man who would call himself *Alter Rex*."

More could not help but breathe a laugh, "Now, now, Harry," he said, shaking his head, "Wolsey was power-hungry, no doubt. The people referred to him as 'The Other King', yes. But surely you know me well enough to know I am a humble man, caring little for fortunes and glory. I speak only, as you must know, my thoughts. And you know my thoughts. If you do not seek my advice, then why call for me at all?"

It was true. Thomas More was a humanist of the simplest forms, a man who was known for his chosen poverty in service of the Catholic church. King Henry was aware of More's aversion of his recent goals to be rid of Katherine and to denounce the pope's ruling.

But Henry also respected More's opinion, as well as his friendship. He only wished More would finally see it as he did: that one could continue as a Catholic at heart, yet still go against the pope's judgement.

"Wolsey failed," Henry concluded, choosing not to answer More's questions and reasoning, "And regardless as to why the man died, he is dead. I shall have to be satisfied with that."

More shook his head again, disappointed in his king, "You asked the impossible of the man."

"Ach!" Henry rasped, throwing his hand in the air and turning away, "It shall *not* be impossible! One way or another I shall gain a male successor."

More did not even flinch, so accustomed was he to the king's outbursts, "And have you come to a conclusion as to which bride ought to replace Queen Katherine yet? Is your heart still set on the Mistress Anne? Or is Bessie Blount and your son Lord Richmond to be your choice?"

Henry narrowed his eyes at More, deliberating, same as he had done for months. Then he jerked his chin at his advisor.

"What do you think I should do?" he asked, his voice so quiet that More was reminded of a time when King Henry was but a young man of eighteen. Green at reigning as well as at life.

Thomas More sighed deeply in thought, though he already knew his answer, "Does it matter what *I* think?"

Henry rubbed his hand over his face, his stubble scratching at his palm, "My need for Anne is strong, Thomas," he admitted, "I am not sure you or anyone can understand. She makes me *crazy*!"

"As I recall, the Lady Blount once made you crazy."

Henry shook his head, sat down on the lounger opposite More, "Not like this," he said, "I have never felt this desperate for anyone."

"And this thirst," More pondered, "it is not but her insistence that you cannot have her until you are wed?"

The king ran his hands through his copper hair, "I no longer know!" he said with a groan.

"Then perhaps it is best you do not proceed with the Boleyn girl," More concluded, "If it is indeed but a son you seek, Bessie is the safest option."

Chapter 11

January 1531

For the New Year celebrations and gift-giving, King Henry and his former mistress Bessie Blount gave their son a joint gift of a ship shaped frankincense container in a silver gilt engraved with the initials 'H+E', for Henry and Elizabeth.
And the gossip that followed spread through the court like wildfire.
"The King has chosen his son's mother."
"King Henry has tired of Mistress Anne."
"Bessie Blount is to be our future queen."
The whispers were uncontrollable.
Henry Fitzroy, who had remained at court to finish his education while also attending Parliament in the House of Lords, was not so easily beguiled by the rumours.
Now at the age of almost twelve, he had grown up an intelligent, competitive and hot-headed young man, one who revelled in athletic pastimes – much like his father – especially jousting and archery. It was because of his shrewdness that he did not believe the new web of lies the courtiers were spinning, no matter how the joint gift would appear as proof to most.
And yet, he did not wish to quash the talk either, his chest filling with pride to think that the people believed that he *could* one day amount to so much.
As well as the beautiful frankincense, the following day Henry also received a lavish gift from the Mistress Anne – which only strengthened his reasoning that she had not, in fact, fallen out of favour with the king to be replaced with Henry's mother. For why would she be gifting her supposed rival's son something as extravagant as a horse if she were at all in competition with him and his mother for the king's affection?

"A horse?" Henry asked, dumbfounded by her generosity after most of the court had gathered out in the courtyard to bear witness to the surprise.

The lady smiled prettily, and Henry was reminded of how her plain face lit up with joy.

"A stallion," she added with a delicate nod of her head.

"I thank you," the boy admitted sincerely, bowing his head at her in appreciation before walking over to where the steed was being held by the reins by a stable boy.

It was a magnificent beast, Henry noted as he approached, with black fur as slick as the night sky, and a pink muzzle, the only other colour on the dark animal.

Henry raised his hand, his palm flat as he had been taught when he was but four, and pressed it gently to its soft mouth, to show that he was not a threat. But instead of lapping at his palm with its big lips, it snorted suddenly, raising its head up and its eyes showing the whites.

"It's alright," Henry muttered, frowning slightly. But the stallion reared its head back again, only stopping short due to how the stable boy held the reins taut.

"He's temperamental," the lad warned Henry softly, looking over his shoulder to cast a glance at where the Mistress Anne, the king, and courtiers were standing as they watched and chattered amongst themselves, ignorant to the stallion's spooked reaction.

"Temperamental?" Henry asked, only half listening as he wondered if he could saddle up and head out for a ride later that day. He doubted it, the snow had fallen heavily the day before, and the rain during the night had caused a slush in the fields.

The stable boy nodded, "I told her so," he muttered, "I urged her against choosin' this one."

Henry's attention snapped to the boy then, but before he could ask him to elaborate, the king's voice hollered from behind him.

"We ought to take our steeds out for a ride sometime this week, my boy," he called, to which Henry turned and grinned, knowing it would never happen. King Henry was many things, but he was not as hands-on a father as he liked to pretend. And a *pang* of sadness gripped his heart to think of Gil, whose sudden death continued to grieve him.

The king and his court returned inside then, the courtyard's exposure being far less appealing than the warmth that they would find back indoors in the great hall.

Henry turned back to the young man holding the horse steady.

"You said you warned the Mistress Anne against gifting me this horse?"

The boy swallowed, nodded slightly.

"Why?" Henry asked, "What is the matter with it?"

"It is a beauty," the boy said, "No doubt. She purposefully selected it for its looks. But it is easily spooked, and not well for ridin'."

Henry frowned, "Nonsense," he disagreed, "The Mistress Anne would surely not gift me such a useless beast. I need only gain its trust."

The young man bowed, "Apologies, my lord. You are right of course."

March 1531

The weather had finally turned.

The days had grown longer, the gardens were blooming with colour, and the air was thick with bird and bug song.

And by this time, Henry had been hoping to be on good enough terms with his 'temperamental' mount to take it out for a hunt.

"How fares his mood today?" Henry asked as he stepped foot into the stables, as he had done each week in order to allow the animal to get to know his face, voice and smell.

"No better than last week," one of the men shovelling manure called over, "My lord," he added quickly.

Henry frowned, he had never known a horse to be this bad-tempered.

The first week after receiving it as a New Year's gift from the Mistress Anne, Henry had visited it every day to feed it apples from his palm or to brush it down at the end of the day. He had been around horses long enough to know that some just needed a little extra attention before they let their guard down. Most couldn't care less who rode them or when. But some did, and Henry – as a keen rider – was not opposed to working for a horse's affection.

But *this?* This one was pushing his limits.

"How is he?" Henry asked now, referring to the incident of last week, where the stallion had kicked one of the stable boys with its back leg, only barely missing Henry.

The man scoffed, side-eyeing the stallion, "Black an' blue all down 'is thigh. He was lucky it weren't 'is face! He'd be dead, no doubt."

Henry frowned up at the steed, who he had yet to name. In truth, he didn't care enough for the beast to label it, to lay claim to it with a title. And more recently, Henry had strongly been considering getting rid of it.

"Has he hurt someone else?" Henry asked, taking a tentative step towards the animal and carefully laying a hand on its soft neck. He stroked it, all the while keeping an eye on the animal's face, who had turned slightly to him, as though gauging if it could reach over and bite him.

"Just this mornin' it attacked one of the king's 'orses," the man said now, before calling over to another stable hand for something.

Henry watched the men exchange words, pass each other shovels. Another man carrying a saddle walked past, and Henry looked at it longingly. He'd love nothing better than to take this great beauty out for a morning ride.

He looked at it, at the sheer size of it, all muscle and strength underneath its black velvet coating.

It wasn't worth it, Henry decided as he took a step back, assessing the beast one last time. This monster could easily fling him off and trample him. By the way it was looking at

Henry, its eyes wide, its head bobbing anxiously, he had no doubt the beast had already sized him up. At least, it certainly felt like it had.

April 1531

"I have regifted the stallion the Mistress Anne gave me," Henry informed his father once the animal was exported off the royal grounds.

King Henry and Fitzroy were strolling along the gardens, the king having invited his only son for a spot of archery that morning but having chosen against it on account of the change in weather. A gust of wind whipped past them, almost as if to prove they had made the right decision.

"Whatever for?" the king asked, "It was a fine steed!"

"Indeed," Henry agreed, "It was a looker. But its temperament was not favourable."

"How so?"

Henry raised his eyebrows, two pale red, almost invisible tufts, identical to his father's own, "It kicked at stable boys, almost broke one's damned leg! It would attack the other stallions, and I did not trust it to allow me to ride it."

The king laughed, "It needed but breaking in."

Henry frowned, "And you would have wished for me to do that, would you, Lord Father?"

At that, the king cleared his throat, "Well, no."

They walked on, a silence befalling them as the king considered the information.

Walking past the fountain, Henry observed the ripples on the surface of the water as the wind continued to blow. Leaves flew up into the air, the rustling sounding loud against the quiet that grew between father and son.

"I trust Anne knew nothing of the horse before gifting it to you," King Henry finally said, breaking the silence.

"Of course," his son agreed, though he was not so sure, since gifting a horse presupposed it had been tested for its qualities and breeding.

I urged her against choosing this one.

The king was nodding, his face contorted in thought, and Henry wondered if he, too, was coming to the same conclusion. But then he raised his head and clapped Henry on the shoulder.

"Never fear," he said, "I shall get you another, a better, steed. Now, I have other matters to discuss with you, my boy."

Young Henry gave his father his full attention.

"It is the matter of Parliament," King Henry said.

Ah yes, Henry thought, *the scandalous title*.

"Have the clergy agreed?" the boy asked.

The king had most recently come to the conclusion that he need no longer ask the pope for his ruling on the matter of his annulment. With the guidance of his beloved Anne Boleyn, who had gifted him a book by William Tyndale called 'The Obedience of the Christian Man', he had seen the light when a passage of it stated quite clearly that a king should not be answerable to the pope but *only* to God.

And with that new, and rather coincidental, perspective, the king had then gone on to declare to Parliament earlier in the year that he shall henceforth be titled as Supreme Head of the English Church and Clergy.

Many of the clergy did not agree, of course, to which the king had responded by accusing them of praemunire – the offense of deciding upon English legal cases outside of England – which of course they were, since the outcome of the king's marriage to the queen was a question for the pope in Rome.

But in their fear of punishment, the clergy had pled for a pardon, just as King Henry knew they would, and he – in his generosity – granted them it, on the condition that they name him as Supreme Head of the English Church and Clergy.

Henry Fitzroy – and indeed most of the court – would have been appalled by the level of manipulation used to achieve his goal, if it hadn't been so utterly brilliant.

"The clergy have agreed and been pardoned," the king admitted, the side of his mouth pulling up into a smirk, "They have henceforth accepted the title, but it is yet to be confirmed by Parliament. And this could take months, if not years. But the wheels are in motion, son."
The boy nodded in approval, as he knew he should.
"And Queen Katherine?" he asked.
His father shot him a look, "Do not call her that!"
"Forgive me," Henry replied quickly, "Old habits."
"Katherine continues to refuse acceptance of what is right in front of her. But soon she will understand."
Henry's brows twitched, "How, Lord Father?"
The king straightened his back, "I have made arrangements to finally get through to her how serious I am about this," he said, "And soon, she will wish she had accepted the offer to retire to a nunnery. For when I am done with her, she will grovel and beg at my feet that I make her that offer once more."

July 1531

"Lord Richmond," a messenger said suddenly, breaking Henry's concentration, "The king sends his instructions for the morrow."
He handed Henry a note, which he read immediately, nodding in confirmation.
He and his sister Elizabeth were playing chess at an outdoor stone table marked with the sixty-four black and white squares. It was a glorious summer day, with not a cloud in the sky and a cooling breeze rustling the trees, and Henry had invited his darling sister to spend the afternoon with him before the court departed for summer progress the following day.
Henry peered up at the messenger, "Thank you."
The boy bowed and turned, leaving them alone once more.
"Mother and I will return to our home in Kyme when court leaves," Elizabeth said as she watched Henry fold the note and tuck it into his breast pocket, "As agreed."

Henry exhaled out his nose, then nodded before grabbing his cup of wine and taking a sip.

"Is the queen still none the wiser?" she asked, as if he'd spoken. But he hadn't needed to. She, and the rest of those in the know, had already been sufficiently informed of the king's controversial plan.

Henry moved his bishop, taking Elizabeth's rook, "Check," he said. Then, "The queen has no idea. She and Princess Mary are in for quite the shock."

Elizabeth frowned down at the game, moved her queen to defend the king.

"This game is unrealistic," she said suddenly, noting that fact for the first time.

Henry breathed an unamused laugh, "I'd call it ironic, personally," he said, then knocked Elizabeth's queen aside with his knight, "Checkmate."

Elizabeth sat back in a huff, and the two siblings stared down at the game, both of them with an anxious expression.

Neither of them – nor most of the nobles – were in agreement with what the king had planned, and it had left a sour taste in their mouths ever since the private announcement. And yet, they would do as they were told, of course, lest the king turn his back on them, too.

"Although," Elizabeth said pensively then, picking up her defeated queen. She twirled it around her fingers, "Maybe not so unrealistic. After all, the queen does all the fighting. And she is still always the one who puts herself at risk while the king hides behind others or flees. The queen is always the one to fall first. The king is a coward."

Henry's eyebrows twitched upward, unsure about the comparison, for though he disagreed with their father's treatment of his wife, he would never go so far as to belittle him thusly. And certainly not out loud.

"Well…" he said, feeling as though he should defend his father from Elizabeth's opinion, for fear of being overheard.

"It is as mother said," Elizabeth interrupted hotly, before he got the chance to speak, "It is a man's world. And we women are but allowed to live in it."

The following day, as arranged, King Henry VIII and the court left on summer progress for the first time in English history without the crowned Queen of England.
She, as well as their daughter Princess Mary, were left ignorant of the king's plans to leave them behind, only receiving the news after the fact, as though they were no more than kitchen maids left behind to clean up the court's mess.
Royal progresses were a vital part of the monarch's reign, as it allowed for the king and queen to be seen by their people and to remind the citizens of their power, strength and divinity. It was an official event which occurred several times throughout each year, the king's huge household travelling through cities and towns and staying at other noble residences.
And so, to blatantly organise such a public event *without* the Queen Consort – and with the king's favourite by his side instead – showed the country that, as far as Henry VIII was concerned, Anne Boleyn was his queen, and no other.
It was quite the outlandish spectacle, many common folk feeling hurt and betrayed to see their king disrespect their queen so. For it was one thing to hear whispers and rumours of the goings on at court and of the way the queen was being mistreated. But it was quite another thing entirely to witness it with their own eyes. And the people were not alone in their upset, many lords and ladies of the court having been shocked to receive the news of their departure without their queen.
But there was nothing anyone could do. Henry VIII had set the wheels in motion to replace his wife in whatever way he could. And since she had made it clear that she would not be willing to remove herself from court, King Henry saw no other way but to remove the court from her.

*

King Henry had left behind instructions for Katherine of Aragon to have left Windsor by the time he returned from the summer progress, and for their daughter Mary to henceforth no longer be allowed any contact with her mother, not even through letters.

It had not been a pretty sight, the two women's reaction to be separated so cruelly. But they did as they were told, just the same as they had always done.

For while it broke their hearts to be torn apart, likely never to see each other again, the queen and princess were loyal to their king.

It was a strange feeling, loving and admiring one's father and yet believing them to be doing wrong.

Henry, who had seen firsthand how a loving relationship should be through his mother and stepfather's marriage, felt unsettled to continuously see his father cast aside his most loyal and devoted wife so disturbingly. Especially when the nobles and the people had so ardently proven their acceptance of not only the king's legitimate daughter as his heir, but even of him, an illegitimate son.

Surprisingly, the king had made him – the child who had previously been in direct competition with Queen Katherine and her daughter – feel a kind of kinship for them. For they were all three now being pushed aside for the mere *hope* of greener pastures.

It made young Henry feel uncomfortable, as though he were somehow betraying his father for not agreeing with his actions, and for suddenly siding with his own former foe.

But there was nothing he could do. Not that he would ever do something even if he could, for like the king's wife and daughter, Henry would remain loyal to his sovereign's wishes. Regardless of his own downfall.

Loyalty was a strange thing like that.

But in the safety of his own mind, Henry allowed himself to learn from his father's woeful behaviour, and he vowed not to follow in his footsteps as a husband, a father, or even a king. For underneath the jewels, the titles, and the power, Henry realised, King Henry VIII was not a man worth admiring.

Chapter 12

August 1532

Though he chose to ignore it, King Henry was reviled both at home and abroad for his gross mistreatment of his loyal and devoted wife and legitimate daughter.
This had been made clear during the summer progress of the previous year, when Henry had left Queen Katherine behind and flaunted the Mistress Anne to the people in order to gauge their acceptance of her as their new queen.
It had not gone as he'd hoped.
In many of the towns, small folk had lined up to hurl insults at the couple, pleading the king to return to his true wife before scurrying away into the crowd. Some had even thrown stones at the woman who would call herself queen, and Henry had had to abruptly end the tour.
Upon their return to London, Henry had gone on as though nothing untoward had happened during the progress, choosing instead to celebrate the fact that Katherine of Aragon was no longer among them at court. Just as he had bid her not to be.
Now, a year on, the king would continue to turn a blind eye to his country's hostility towards his chosen bride, deciding instead to lay titles and land at her feet, in order to elevate her in any way he could.
For, as he had learned in the case of his bastard son, anyone could be accepted so long as they were raised high enough. Because when it was all said and done, popularity came down to one crucial detail: presentation.

September 1532

Archbishop William Warham, who had filled this role since before Henry VIII's coronation, had suddenly died the previous month.

At the age of eighty-two, it had come as no surprise, and without much ado, King Henry had installed his replacement: someone who would further aid him on his quest.

"No doubt the new Archbishop Thomas Cranmer will get my father what he wants," Henry Fitzroy admitted to his close friend Hal, who, now at fifteen, had grown into a boisterous young man. But for all his rowdiness, Hal had remained a loyal friend to Henry, unlike George who had distanced himself in favour of men his own age now that he was old enough to revoke lessons altogether.

Good riddance, Henry had confided in Hal when George had gravitated away from them. And he and Hal had grown closer for George's absence.

"Indeed," Hal agreed now, "Cranmer is renowned for his keenness for the reformation."

"And he is friendly with your cousins, the Boleyns," thirteen-year-old Henry added.

"Of course."

Henry nodded in thought as the two young men turned the corner to the great hall, where the most recent event was to take place.

"What your father wants," Hal said cautiously then, having noticed his friend's recent unease, "It is not what you want?"

Henry stopped abruptly, pulling Hal by the arm towards the wall. He looked around himself, waited a moment as a group of nobles walked past, muttering under their breaths.

"Of course it is what I want!" the boy feigned, "Whatever is the king's wish is also mine."

Hal nodded, one dark eyebrow raised, "Naturally."

"It is just –" Henry cleared his throat, turning his back to the guards nearby, "The woman does not like me."

Again, Hal nodded. He had heard of this before, through court gossip as well as Henry's own beliefs.

"The stallion," Hal surmised.

Henry nodded, "Yes, the stallion. What kind of gift is that? Had I been boastful and decided to ride it that day, it may have killed me."

"She cannot have known," Hal offered in defence of his cousin.

Laughter trickled out from the great hall as courtiers had begun to gather for the occasion. Henry turned his head towards it, then back to Hal.

"You're right," he replied, choosing to agree, "It is but a morbid fancy of mine."

"After today's elevation, she will be the most prestigious non-royal woman in the realm."

Henry straightened up, raised his chin before entering the great hall, "I know."

Hal, as ever, followed behind.

"With the new title of Marquess of Pembroke, the Mistress Boleyn will become Lady Boleyn. She will be queen in all but name."

"I know," Henry repeated, his stomach tightening at the prospect, for with Anne Boleyn's elevation, Henry couldn't help but feel suddenly overlooked.

His stepfather's words echoed in his mind then.

Your success dampens her own.

And he realised it was true the other way around, too.

He looked about the vast rooms, searching for his mother and sister's familiar faces.

"With Cranmer in office," Hal continued, leaning closer to his friend, "It is only a matter of time before your father gains his annulment. After that, who knows how long you shall remain the king's only son. You would do well to establish yourself. Look for a way to make your worth shine brighter. Perhaps stop waiting for things to fall into your lap and grab the bull by the horns."

And with that he broke off and headed towards his father the Duke of Norfolk who stood by the fire with a handful of other nobles.

Henry watched him go, a frown etched between his brows to think his friend, who was the Mistress Anne's cousin, would give him advice for his own success rather than to defer him, and thereby clearing the way for Anne to obtain the throne that much easier.

He smiled briefly to realise Hal was a true friend.

Either that, or he was playing both sides carefully, in the event that either one of them landed on top.

With the momentum that he felt following Anne Boleyn's elevation to Marquess and Thomas Cranmer's promotion to Archbishop of Canterbury, King Henry VIII made arrangements to meet with Francis I of France in the hope that he would aid his cause further.

"Francis I needs us," Henry explained to his council as if they didn't already know, "His continued strife with Charles V of Spain shall work in my favour when I come to ask him what I would want in return for our support."

"And what is that, Your Highness?" William Fitzwilliam asked, his quill at the ready in case he would need to take notes. William Fitzwilliam had recently replaced Thomas More as Lord Chancellor and advisor to Henry VIII, More having resigned shortly after Cranmer's election to Archbishop.

I cannot stand by and assist you on this quest, Harry! It goes against God, and I shall not support it.

The king had let him go, for now, since Henry no longer cared to hear his alternate counsel.

"During the arranged meeting at Boulogne and Calais," the king said, to which the French ambassador nodded once in confirmation, "Francis I shall receive myself and Lady Anne as a couple, officially giving us his kingly seal of approval."

The advisors nodded slowly, so far they knew of these preparations.

"And having no cardinal of my own currently," the king went on, his face darkening at the slight mention of Wolsey, "I shall request that King Francis afford me the use of his cardinals in the Vatican to plead my case with the pope once more for a formal annulment of my marriage."

Fitzwilliam nodded, though his dark eyebrows were bunched together so tightly they were nearly touching.

"The pope has already threatened to excommunicate Your Majesty if you were to continue your pursuit of the Lady Anne," Charles Brandon reminded him, "Do you really suppose asking *again* for an annulment would be in aid of anything?"

King Henry slammed his hands down on the wooden table. None but Fitzwilliam flinched.

"Goddammit, Charles!" Henry shouted, "I shall ask again and again until he gives me what I want or until he does *indeed* excommunicate me! Whichever comes first. Until Parliament passes the Act naming me Supreme Head of the Church of England, I *must* continue to beg His Holiness for it!"

Charles raised his hands in surrender but remained cool. He was not fazed by his friend's outbursts, having witnessed more than he could count in recent years. By now, they had lost their sting.

"Any other points you would wish to broach to the King of France?" Fitzwilliam asked.

"Yes," the king replied, his anger gone as easily as it had come, "One final point. I wish to take my son with me, to introduce him to Francis and to ask him to let him join the French Court."

"You think King Francis will agree?" Charles enquired, genuinely uncertain.

"Of course!" Henry assured, "Why on Earth wouldn't he!?"

The trip to Calais was intended to introduce Anne Boleyn to the European stage as England's future queen consort.

King Francis, though he himself was a Catholic who answered to the pope, would feign being delighted to receive the King of England and his courtesan, for he would receive vastly more in return from them than he would have to give. All King Henry had really asked for, was to publicly accept the Lady Anne. And while he did not see the big problem with that, he would soon come to realise that when it came to the ladies of France, Anne Boleyn was not viewed as an ally.

Francis found it all rather amusing, to say the least, for he knew Anne Boleyn well, she and her sister Mary Boleyn having spent many years in the French court when they had been ladies-in-waiting to his wife Queen Claude. He had found her very interesting: a clever and witty lady. She had turned many heads during her time in France. But it had been her sister who Francis had taken to his bed.

In truth, Francis found King Henry's obsession with the less beautiful of the two Boleyn sisters more than a little peculiar. Anne was not the kind of woman *he* would personally choose. For a mistress *or* a wife. Too clever for his liking. Francis enjoyed his women quiet and subservient. And by the way she was making Henry VIII run around, making him wait to marry her before he could have her...well, she clearly had control over him. And that was not something Francis would exactly be promoting in *his* court.

But, for the sake of appearances and his need for England's support of his war on Spain – as well as for the respect he had for the woman, for she was playing a daring and quite unique game – he would receive them.

The only problem was that no noble lady would do the same.

"Few believe the Lady to be a virgin," King Francis' ambassador explained, though Francis had heard all these rumours before, "She is seen throughout the French court as King Henry VIII's mistress, usurping the rightful place of a good and pious queen who has strong international ties."

But the French King did not care, because he *needed* England's support for his cause.

Francis I realised, however, that it would be increasingly difficult to find any royal lady who would wish to receive Anne Boleyn.

"Henry and Anne are shameful," Queen Eleanor had said, refusing. But then again, she *was* Katherine of Aragon's niece, Francis thought.

However, King Francis' sister, Marguerite – who was a close friend of Anne Boleyn's from her time in France – had also gone on to refuse, saying that, "As Queen of Navarre I cannot be associated with the 'Scandal of Christendom'."

Scandal of Christendom, that was what Anne Boleyn was being referred to as in the royal women's circle.

And so, with a chuckle, King Francis thought of another option.

"He suggests his own mistress," the French ambassador now told Henry VIII, reading the missive from his king aloud, "to greet Your Majesty's mistress when she is to arrive in Calais."

"Anne is not my mistress," Henry muttered, stunned by King Francis' offer.

"Is there no other?" Charles Brandon asked, feigning horror, though he had expected such an outcome. Anne Boleyn was not exactly well liked. Neither in England, nor, it seemed, even in France.

"No noble lady, not even Princess Marguerite, has accepted." The news came as a blow to the King of England. His elevation of the lady had not yet worked to alter the people's perception of her.

But in true Henry VIII fashion, he would not be deterred.

October 1532
Staple Inn, Calais, France

The trip from Dover to Calais was but five hours long, the wind behind them spurring them ahead; but, ashamedly, Henry Fitzroy had become queasy, nonetheless.

Never having sailed on a ship before, he had, at first, marvelled at the ocean, at the ship as it sliced through the water, at the seagulls *cawing* above them. But soon enough the young man had retired below deck to lie down, having failed to find his sea legs. Thankfully, Henry thought later, his father had been too preoccupied with his plans and his beloved to notice.

When they arrived in France, King Henry decided to leave Anne Boleyn behind on English territory of Calais, while he went to Boulogne, France, to meet King Francis; since no royal lady had agreed to receive her.

For four days he attended the French court, where extravagant feasts were held each night and discussions of their new Anglo-French alliance were had.

His son Henry Fitzroy had accompanied him to Boulogne, the thirteen-year-old boy shadowing his father throughout the visit to learn the ways of kings by osmosis.

"Ah, he is strong and tall," King Francis had said upon their first meeting. He'd clapped the young man on the back in a way which young Henry could only assume was meant to both placate and intimidate him. As though to make his mark as the alpha on the potential next King of England – or Ireland.

"The ladies, they swoon to behold you, Lord Richmond," King Francis had grinned mischievously, giving Henry the sense that, at his age, the French King was already well versed on women and their bodies.

"The apple doesn't fall far from the tree," Henry's father had added, and the two men had guffawed companionably.

To his shame, young Henry had flushed at the remarks, for he had yet to know the touch of a woman. Not that he had paid the opposite sex that much attention – at thirteen he was only just becoming aware of such things.

"Ah, look at him blush," King Francis had said, "He is in dire need of France to pull him out of his shell! Lest he become a rigid Englishman! The boy may stay!"

The two kings had laughed together again, though Henry had been astutely aware that his father's laugh was no longer genuine. For though Henry VIII had gained one of the things he had wanted from this trip – his son's invitation to remain at French court – it had been at the expense of his bruised ego.

Henry had been glad to see the end of the short stay in Boulogne and to return to Calais, where the English court awaited them. Being presented to the French court as King Henry VIII's most precious jewel had been an honour, no doubt. But the constant parading over those four days had taken its toll. And Henry could only hope that once his father and household would depart for English shores and leave Henry behind, that he would find his footing more easily without his father's constant vaunting of him.

"It's good to be back," Henry admitted to his good friend Hal now, having freshened up after their sumptuous arrival procession into Calais.

"Too much politics?" Hal asked with a grin.

"Too much boasting."

The two young men chuckled as they made their way to the banquet.

"Has King Francis agreed to speak for your father on his matter to the pope?" Hal enquired, dropping his voice slightly on account of the sensitive topic.

Henry shook his head, "I am not certain it has been discussed yet," he admitted, "Not in my presence, at least."

Hal nodded slowly, and the two of them entered the hall.

Lit warmly by dozens of soft flickering candles in wrought-iron sconces, the air carried a smoky scent of burning wood and the faint body odour of the hundreds of courtiers within it. It held an intimate warmth, the flickering firelight from the vast hearth in the far corner lending a golden glow to the walls and floors which were decorated with silk tapestries and cloth of gold carpeting.

With the two kings seated at the high table, the courtiers – both English and French – lounged around the room, gossiping, drinking and laughing as they awaited the entertainment which they knew was to follow.

Henry and Hal took a seat at the long table just beyond the royal canopy, underneath which King Henry and King Francis sat at the high table. Beside King Francis was his beautiful, dark-haired mistress, while the seat beside King Henry remained unoccupied.

Henry turned his attention to his plate of food, and waited for the dramatic entrance which he knew was to come, for it had been a matter of much discussion among the courtiers.

After a moment, the music changed to initiate the performance and Henry looked up.

She and the seven ladies who accompanied her were dressed in a strange fashion, Henry noted, made of cloth of gold, compassed with crimson tinsel satin and joined with cloth of silver and knitted with laces of gold.

Like a Greek goddess, the boy realised.

Along with her ladies – her sister Mary Boleyn just behind her – the group danced for the King of France and the court. They wore masks to hide their features, but everyone knew which one among them was the charismatic Anne Boleyn, for she exuded an allure unlike any other, her expressive eyes and elegant movements standing out.

Each lady broke away from the centre then and chose a partner to dance with, the leading lady selecting King Francis.

It came as a surprise to no one, after the dance ended and the ladies removed their masks, that the King of France had been dancing with the Lady Anne Boleyn. But he feigned surprise nonetheless, to appease the crowd.

"Where are they going?" Hal asked Henry then, as King Francis took Anne by the hand and escorted her to a private corner of the hall.

Henry, who had returned his attention to the courtiers before him after the reveal, followed Hal's gaze.

"I'm not sure," he said, "But it can't be anything sinister. My father is right there. No doubt it is all part of the plan. Part of the formal acknowledgment of the lady."

Hal nodded, then sighed contentedly and picked up the cup before him.

"France, eh?" he sighed, sitting back in his seat and casting a look over a group of ladies giggling and gossiping at a table nearby.

"We are not in France," Henry reminded him, picking up his own cup and raising it for a servant to refill, "Calais is ours."

Hal laughed, flashing his crooked front teeth, "I do not speak of the ground we walk on," he lifted his cup, and his eyebrow, to a young French woman across the room, who smiled seductively back at Hal.

Henry shook his head, though he felt an uncomfortable warmth creeping up his neck and cheeks.

He did not reply, turning back to look at where King Francis and Anne Boleyn had gone off to unchaperoned, instead.

Through the dimly lit archway where they sat, Henry thought he saw the king shaking his head as the lady spoke swiftly, her hands gesticulating before her. It appeared ominous for a moment, but then the two of them threw their heads back and laughed so loudly Henry heard it faintly over the sound of the music and the court's merriment.

Whatever they were discussing, it was positive.

And Henry suddenly realised that Hal had been right: he could no longer simply wait around for his father to name him as heir. If he wanted the throne of England, he would have to make his mark.

Chapter 13

November 1532
Château Amboise, France

Though Francis I had refused to ask his cardinals to speak for King Henry on his Great Matter to the pope, with Francis' tacit seal of approval for their union, Anne and Henry had received part of what they had asked for.
And with that, they departed for England as soon as the weather permitted.
Henry Fitzroy, as agreed upon between the two monarchs, remained behind and joined the French court. His good friend Hal Howard, too.
"I now have four sons!" King Francis had grinned in welcome, accepting him as an English Prince, before admitting him to his Privy Chamber – an incredible honour for a bastard child.
They would henceforth live with the Dauphin of France, named Francis after his father; the boys all being of similar ages. They quickly formed a close connection, bonding over their shared love of horse riding and archery, as well as pulling pranks on one another.
But with Henry Fitzroy's new outlook on his fragile position as the King of England's only son, he would often remind himself to take this new arrangement seriously. His father, before his departure, had secretly instructed Henry to observe the King of France and his advisors while he remained among them, and to report back any interesting gossip to the English ambassador. Henry did not much like the idea of being a spy, and yet he would do as he was asked if it meant he would prove his worth to his father in this small way. With this task he was not actively working against either Queen Katherine or the Lady Anne. And his conscience was clear of that, at least.

"The ladies here," Hal said one day some weeks after King Henry and Anne Boleyn had returned to England, "They are all so...enticing."

Young Henry had nodded, though he'd failed to notice. Too preoccupied was he with his dilemma.

Hal smirked and winked at a lady then as she walked past, her red velvet dress brushing past them as they sat by the fire in the great hall. She smiled back at him with hooded eyes.

Hal sighed, "We are in paradise."

Henry shuffled the deck in his hands and dealt out their cards, "Indeed," he said noncommittally.

Hal sat forward, picked up his cards, "You don't think so?"

Henry looked about himself, as though he were taking in his surroundings for the first time.

Château Amboise's great hall was built in the French Gothic style, covered by stone vaults, its ceilings made of wood and decorated with polychromed carved lattices. On the walls, huge fireplaces contributed to produce a monumental effect. But Henry knew it was not the architecture that Hal was referring to, but rather its occupants.

He cast a glance over the many courtiers, both male and female, dressed in the finest fashions, gossiping in French behind delicate hands. To Henry, they appeared not much different to English courtiers, though he could appreciate that the French had a certain air about them. A more relaxed and – as Hal had said – enticing aura.

"We are in paradise," Henry agreed with Hal, hoping that would put a stop to the conversation.

He fanned out his cards, "I dealt. You begin."

For a moment, the two boys played *Triomphe* in silence, both of them fixated on winning, when Hal broke the silence.

"What about her?" he said, leaning forward to whisper eagerly across the table.

Henry turned in his seat to follow his gaze and saw a pretty noble lady laughing as she and her group crossed the hall and took a seat by the windows.

"What about her?" Henry replied rhetorically.

"She's beautiful."

"And also betrothed," Henry said matter-of-factly, taking a card from the top of the deck.

Hal shrugged, "How do you know that?"

"I don't, really," he replied, "But for a lady of her age and station not to be betrothed is unlikely."

"You aren't betrothed," Hal pointed out.

Henry lifted his gaze, played his turn, "She is older than I, and of marrying age."

Hal chuckled, shaking his head as though he'd said something funny, "Henry."

"What?" the younger boy replied with a frown.

"Any day now, you will wake up and discover the wonders of women. You will see them everywhere, and you will not be able to think of anything but them until your head hits the pillow at night. And even then, in your dreams, you will see them."

Hal looked about himself again, drinking in the many beauties of all ages.

"And when you do," he continued, ignoring Henry's doubtful look, "You will not care that they are betrothed, married, clubfooted or otherwise."

Henry laughed then, "You jest," he said, the 'clubfooted' remark tickling him.

Hal lay down his cards, showing a winning hand, "I do not. And when that day comes, I expect to have a decent conversation with you about the many marvels of the female form."

January 1533

News came from England that his father had finally achieved what he had wished for so long and Henry was torn as to how he felt about it.

"He and the Lady Anne are married, before God," he told his friends Prince Francis and Hal in fluent French, "Archbishop Cranmer proclaimed Anne as the new queen. It is official."

"Has the pope granted King Henry his annulment?" Prince Francis asked, dumbfounded.

Henry looked down at the letter in his hands, "It does not say so here…"

Francis raised his eyebrows at Henry. Despite his father's acknowledgement of Anne Boleyn the previous year, Prince Francis and the whole of the French court – who likely had learned of this development before Henry himself, gossip travelling faster than correspondence – were stunned at this news. For, as a Catholic nation, their ultimate loyalties still lay with the pope.

"It is bigamous then," Prince Francis dismissed, shrugging his shoulders, "It is not legal."

"But it has been accepted," Hal interjected, frowning.

"It is a scandal," Prince Francis countered, then looked to Henry, "But a scandal which England accepts, *non*?"

Henry shook his head, flicked a glance at his friend Hal.

"Not so," Henry answered Francis, daring to speak the truth despite his audience, his good friend Hal being related by blood to the new would-be queen meaning that his loyalties may have now shifted slightly in her favour, "There is much dislike for the lady. As a Member of Parliament, I was witness to all who spoke against her. The public openly despises her. Even my father's favourite sister, Mary Tudor Queen of France and her husband Charles Brandon Duke of Suffolk oppose the relationship."

Hal pursed his lips, as Henry knew he would, "And yet she is the queen."

His tone was sharper than Henry had expected from him. But he nodded, understanding the awkward position he was in, same as Henry was, "She is."

"So, it matters not what the public or the nobles think," Hal added, to which Prince Francis straightened his back and inhaled, as though he would disagree.

Francis was bothered by the remark, for the nobles' and the public's love was precisely what *made* a monarch. Without the people's acceptance, the monarchy would surely become obsolete.

But Hal would not understand. Francis and Henry shared a knowing look.

"It is done," Henry concluded, choosing to focus on the small part within him that was delighted for his father's triumph, "And I am glad to see my father achieve his goal. I am but the King of England's subject, and if he is happy, then so am I."

June 1533

It wasn't until five months later that Archbishop Cranmer would be able to annul the marriage between Henry VIII and Katherine of Aragon; during which time, Anne Boleyn's belly grew bigger with each passing month.

Following their leave from Calais back in November of the previous year, Anne Boleyn had finally, after seven long years, given herself to the king. Their coupling had led to a swift conception, which no doubt triggered their need to arrange for a swift wedding back in January, for King Henry could not afford for the infant's legitimacy to be questioned. Since this child may very well be that long sought-after boy the king so craved.

And now, with the queen heavy with child, news came from England that Anne Boleyn had been crowned in a lavish celebration. One that, though glorious, had not been attended by many of the people, the public's unwillingness to accept her as their queen continuing to be made very clear.

Henry Fitzroy couldn't help but secretly gain some satisfaction over this turn of events, feeling a wave of appreciation for the people who appeared to be more willing to accept him than the pretender-queen. Granted, the small folk would – above all else – rather see the Princess Mary be returned to favour and named the king's official heir. But that was very unlikely to ever happen now that their father had gained his annulment and declared his daughter a bastard, just as Henry had always been. In terms of status, Mary was now of no more merit to the king than Henry himself was. And if their gender aided in defining their value – which Henry knew it did – then by all accounts Henry Fitzroy was suddenly of higher esteem than the former Princess of England. And he couldn't imagine how much that must pain his half-sister.

Here in France, they had even taken to referring to him as 'Prince Henry'; a title he may not have been born with, but one the French would grant him nonetheless, clearly suggesting their acceptance of him as a Prince of England.

And yet, it did little to aid the gloom he felt over the fact that his own father would rather continue to hope for better things from Anne Boleyn.

Why couldn't he simply have gained his annulment and focused on the son he *did* have? The son who he himself proclaimed to 'love above all others.'

Henry had done his father's bidding at every opportunity, never once speaking out against his whims. Even when he had been scared to be separated from his family at five years old. Even when he felt sickened at Queen Katherine and Princess Mary's treatment, though he had once viewed them as his rivals. Even when the woman his father had chosen for his new wife appeared not to like him.

Henry's mind was running away from him, his worries and fears taking over the logical part of his brain that told him to simply continue as he had been, for he had never fallen out of favour with his father yet. He inhaled deeply to calm his nerves, made himself listen to his rational mind: as long as he did as he was bid, the king would reward him in one way or another.

And who knew, perhaps the new queen would fail in producing a son, just as the previous queen had.

It *was* entirely possible.

Henry held onto that hope as he made his way to the joust which was scheduled to take place that morning.

The young man lifted his gaze in an attempt to distract himself with his glorious surroundings.

Château Amboise was built delicately above the river and had hedges stretching so high they appeared to touch the sky. He looked up, shielding his eyes from the sun to examine the palace from where he stood. Its former medieval fortress, Henry had been told, provided a great view over the town of Amboise, though he had not yet had the chance to explore it for himself. Henry made a mental note to do so at his next opportunity. Perhaps Prince Francis would show him –

"Who would you put your wager on, Prince Henry?"

The excited French voice jolted him from his thoughts, and he looked over his shoulder to find a young girl grinning eagerly at him, her grey eyes shining with delight for the entertainment to come.

"I ought to bet on my Lord Father, of course. But the other rider, he's a knight, and he is awfully good," she rambled on.

Henry returned her smile. Her jittery excitement was infectious.

He had noticed her before, of course, for it was impossible not to notice the daughter of the King of France when residing at the French court.

"Princess Madeleine," Henry said in greeting, bowing his head at the twelve-year-old girl, "I cannot discuss the matter. It would be treason," he grinned, whispering conspiratorially.

Madeleine of Valois giggled and looped her arm through his, causing him to flinch slightly in surprise.

"So you, too, would bet on the knight, *oui?*" she said.

Henry looked at her, amused, "What brings you here?" he asked then, looking over his shoulder, only to find they were unchaperoned, "Does your governess know where you are?" he asked, a prickling heat crawling up his neck to realise they were alone.

Madeleine *tutted* and waved her hand in the air, a delicate gesture the French women appeared to have perfected, "I snuck out. Jousts are not deemed suitable entertainment for a princess. But they are far more enthralling than embroidery, trust me."

Henry forced a chuckle, "I don't doubt it," and moved slightly in order to unlock their arms, "You should await one of your ladies, perhaps."

Madeleine frowned, but her smile remained, "*Pourquoi*? So they can run off and tell my stepmother of my whereabouts?" she sighed, "Come, you must hide me."

Henry licked his dry lips, looked longingly at the tiltyard in the distance, flags flapping in the breeze above. Many courtiers were making their way towards it from all angles but only a handful had taken the path through the garden as Henry and Madeleine had. And again, their unchaperoned proximity made him uneasy, "I cannot think that would be a good idea," he protested.

She shrugged one delicate shoulder, not noticing his nervousness, "Don't be a spoil sport like my brother," she teased, grabbing hold of his arm.

Henry flinched at the feel of her soft hand in his, and he pulled away, "I have no intention of hiding you."

At that, Madeleine retrieved her hand and her smile, leaving only her frown behind.

"*Alors*," she said, "But do not tell anyone you saw me. I wish not to be discovered."

And with that, she picked up the skirts of her blue silk dress and hurried through the gardens, taking care not to be spotted by anyone who might betray her, and leaving Henry to quash the flush of his cheeks.

He was ashamed to admit that he was infatuated with Princess Madeleine. And the reason why he felt ashamed, was that he did not feel worthy enough to harbour these affections for her.

Henry had been residing at the French court for little over three weeks when the princess had returned from her country residence with her household to reunite with her family for the Christmastide in December.

Back then, Henry had not expected to be interested in female company, the only girl he had ever liked to spend time with being his sister Elizabeth.

Girls usually liked girly things. Dancing, stitching, singing, gossiping. And they were not things Henry cared for as forms of entertainment. Despite his recent realisations about his father, he could still agree with him that archery, jousting, hunting, and hawking were far greater forms of leisure.

But Madeleine had been different, and she'd made that perfectly clear as soon as they had first met.

My sister, Madeleine, Prince Francis had said when she had appeared suddenly from around a corner, racing towards them, her skirts bunched in her fists as she ran.

Brother, she'd said breathlessly, her round face rosy as she looked over her shoulder, *I was never here.*

Princess Madeleine! A voice had called angrily from down the corridor then, and the girl's glee had transformed into horror.

Quick!

Suddenly they were all running, though Henry had had no idea why, where to, or who from.

Bursting through a door and carefully closing it behind them, the three of them had crouched down behind it, Madeleine pressing a finger to her lips.

Henry had frowned at Francis, who shrugged at him as if to say, *Just go with it.*

They'd listened as hastened footsteps hurried past the door, Madeleine's eyes wide at the growing, then fading, sound.

Henry observed her as they sat frozen. She had eyes of pale grey, like that of a cloudy day, and plump, blushing cheeks. Her hair, though underneath a French hood, peaked out at the crown showing a splash of chestnut brown. She was wearing a yellow satin dress with fur trimming on the sleeves, and as Henry continued to survey her, he noticed that the bottom of her dress was wet and muddy.

Have you been down by the river again, Madeleine? Francis had whispered then, as if he'd read Henry's mind, *You know how father hates you going there!*

The rats are huge there, though! Madeleine had hissed back in form of explanation, as if they were not dirty vermin but some treasure to be marvelled at.

Henry's lips had twitched into a surprised smile, and he'd looked at Francis, who had rolled his eyes.

It was from then on that whenever Henry spotted her among the crowd, his hands would get clammy, and his throat would close up. Even to simply hear her laugh, which was loud and brash, made him turn his head towards the sound in the hope of catching a glimpse of her. It was as Hal had told him just two weeks before her arrival at the French court, once he noticed the opposite sex, there would be no going back.

Though it wasn't women in general that he had noticed, no other lady had the ability to quicken his pulse with but a look. Just the one. A mischievous and daring young princess, who cared more for fun than looking pretty.

What he felt was not on par, however, with the lustful yearnings that Hal often spoke of. He did not wish to see what she hid beneath her dress nor what her hand felt like in his. And he wondered if perhaps it was because he was yet too young, or whether what he liked about her was her mind over her body. And yet, sometimes, when they were alone – which was not often given that she had attendants and ladies surrounding her almost constantly – Henry would find his gaze drifting from her eyes to her lips, and an overwhelming desire to kiss her would take over.

He never would, of course. For she was a royal Princess of Valois, and would no doubt soon be married off to some great Prince of Europe, while he was no more than the King of

England's bastard son, who the desperate king did not even deem important enough to legitimise.

But at times, Henry would allow himself to dream. And in his dreams he would be accepted by the people of England and Europe as King Henry's rightful heir. Except now, it was no longer due to the childish belief that the throne of England was his by right as the king's only son, but because it would allow him to lean in, plant a kiss on Madeleine's pink lips, and actually be worthy of her.

Hampton Court Palace, London

It brings me great joy to deliver onto you the news I have gathered from the French court.
It will please you, I expect, to learn that King Francis I and his court have breathed not a negative word against Your Highness since your visit, and that their hatred of Spain and the Holy Roman Emperor continues strong. We have nothing to fear from either of them while they tear at each others' throats.
Moreover, I wish to convey that I carry the honour of having been accepted by the French King and his people as your recognized son by the way they refer to me as not Lord Richmond, but Prince Henry. It brings me great pride to be accepted as such, and I dare say it comes as positive news to you, Your Highness, who has always wished for such a development.
H. Richmond

King Henry grinned as he read the letter, his illegitimate son's acceptance by the French coming, indeed, as wonderful news.

"They dote on him," the king informed his new wife as she picked at the food on the silver plate before her.

She looked up, focusing her piercing eyes at the letter, the news immediately pricking her ears.

"They dote on him?" she asked as casually as she could.

King Henry looked up and folded the letter in half, "France. They refer to my son as 'Prince'."

Queen Anne's dark eyebrows shot up, "They do, do they?" she asked, unable to hide her surprise.

Henry did not notice her tone, for he was too busy skimming over the letter again. He sighed contentedly.

At that, Anne put down her spoon and smoothed the silk of her dress over her growing belly.

King Henry noted the movement – as well as the drop in temperature in the room – and turned to look at her, "Do not fear, sweetheart," he laughed, "Our son is of more value to me than any child I have previously sired. It is merely interesting to learn of Richmond's developments."

Anne smiled, but it did not reach her slightly narrowed eyes.

"You have placed a lot of trust into your bastard son," she said, resuming her picking at the pheasant before her.

Henry frowned, "Of course I have. Why would I not?"

Anne shrugged one delicate shoulder, "You do not fret over his growing support from Catholic France?" she asked, watching him carefully as she brought the spoon to her lips.

The king frowned again, "Fret? It is precisely what I have always wanted! For him to be accepted, so that he may be of use to me."

Anne blinked and raised her eyebrows like the conversation didn't matter anyway, for she knew that it was subtleties like that which would make her husband's mind begin to work.

The king scoffed, irked that she had questioned him.

But, just as she knew he would, the king lay down the letter, turned to stare into the embers and considered her warning.

July 1533
Château Amboise, France

"You know she is of delicate health."

Henry, Prince Francis, and Hal were sitting side by side at a banquet as laughter and music swirled around them.

Henry, with a belly full of good French food and wine, had been watching the courtiers' merriment from his seat, occasionally stealing what he thought were subtle glances at Madeleine as she sat with her stepmother Queen Eleanor and a handful of their ladies. She'd just squeezed her eyes shut as a bout of laughter escaped her, Queen Eleanor covering her mouth as she tried to contain her own amusement at the story they were being told, when Prince Francis had pulled him out of his daze with the remark.

Henry turned to look at his friend, "Who?" he asked, not even sure if he was feigning naivety or if he was hoping Francis would name someone else.

Instead, Francis cocked his head to one side, "It is why she is not yet betrothed," he said knowingly, "She was supposed to marry James V of Scotland, but was deemed of too fragile health, so another was suggested."

Henry nodded slowly. Had he been caught out?

"It is why you observe her, *non*?" the prince asked, "Because you fear for her well-being?"

Henry's mouth twitched, relieved his secret may yet be unknown.

"It is," he admitted, "Though I was not aware that she suffered with ill health."

"Oh, *oui*," Francis said, frowning, "Father does not think she would have survived being shipped to Scotland. I hear it is wet and cold and dark."

Henry nodded and looked over his shoulder at the pale princess. Her cheeks were rosy, as ever, but suddenly Henry viewed them no longer as a pretty feature but as a telltale sign of a body that ran too hot, as though constantly fighting off some minor complaint. And yet he could not help but find them beautiful.

"Yes," he said, "Scotland is known for its wet weather."

"But England, especially the south where the English court resides, is much warmer," this from Hal, who had been quietly observing the exchange. He smiled knowingly at Henry now, "Isn't that right, Henry?"

Henry grabbed the opportunity, and his cup of wine, "Oh yes," he said, "It is nowhere near as dreary as I hear Scotland can be."

Prince Francis nodded, though he seemed no longer to care about the subject.

He sighed, bored, "Well, who knows. Maybe my father will yet arrange a marriage for her to some English lord."

He drank from his cup, before standing from his seat and beckoning a lady to dance.

And Henry sat back and smiled, allowing the warm feeling of hope to spread through him.

Chapter 14

Château Amboise, France

"Deal me in," she said as she plonked herself into a chair beside Henry and her brother, tucking her dress underneath the table, "*S'il vous plait*," she added then, smiling prettily.
Henry and Francis exchanged a look, then Francis grabbed the deck in the middle of the table and dealt out a hand for her.
"*Merci,*" she muttered, grabbing the cards and examining them.
"What are we playing?" she asked, glancing briefly over her shoulder.
"Are you hiding from *Madame* again?" Prince Francis asked. Madeleine grinned without looking away from the cards before her, and Henry couldn't help but chuckle. The bubble of contentment as to her company, as well as her sassiness, bursting in his chest.
"It isn't funny, Henry," his friend retorted as he lay down a card and picked up another, "She will get us all in trouble."
Madeleine turned her face to Henry then, as though to judge his opinion on the matter. He felt her gaze on him and braved himself to meet it, ignoring the prickle of warmth climbing up his neck.
Her grey eyes and his blue locked for but a second before both parties returned their attention to the game and Henry took his turn. But in that brief moment he had felt it – at least he hoped he had – that buzz of equal understanding. That they both harboured something for the other beyond friendship.
"You will not rat me out, will you brother?" she asked as she picked up the ace of clubs Henry had discarded and placed down a card of her own.
Henry watched her hand hold onto his card, pretended she was touching it exactly where he had.

Francis sighed and shrugged, "I do not care enough," he admitted.

At that, Madeleine smirked, "I might have guessed as much," she said, then turned her beaming face at Henry, "*Et toi?*" she challenged, "Will you tell *Madame* that I was here if she comes searching for me?"

Henry opened his mouth to speak when he felt her leg press against his under the table, and his words choked in his throat. It was only the slightest touch, but it had caused a riot in the young man's mind, boggling his thoughts. He tried to speak.

Prince Francis looked up from his cards then, "You alright, my friend?" he asked, and Madeleine retracted her leg away from Henry's swiftly.

Henry looked from Madeleine to Francis, concerned that his face was as bright as a glowing ember.

"Fine," he squeaked, then cleared his throat. He was vaguely aware of Madeleine pressing her lips together to stop from giggling.

"I am fine," Henry repeated, before exhaling curtly, regaining his composure and laying down his hand, "But I believe I may have won," and he focused his gaze on Madeleine, whose lips stretched into a slow smile.

August 1533

It was not to be, for after just eleven months at the French court, Henry Fitzroy would be recalled back to England to marry a lady whom he had never met.

"Mary Howard?" Henry asked rhetorically, "Your own sister, Hal."

Mary Howard, who was born the same year as Henry himself, was the youngest daughter of the Duke of Norfolk, sister to Hal, and of course, cousin to the new Queen of England Anne Boleyn. She was a young lady of good connections and of marginally high status. And yet, as the son of the king, Henry found himself wondering why his father would want to marry him off to a mere courtier, when he could have pursued a betrothal to a Princess of Valois.

"You knew nothing about this?" Henry asked his friend Hal, who too was disappointed to learn of their abrupt return to England.

Hal raised his hands, palms forward, "Nothing," he swore, "I am as baffled as you. When do we leave?"

Henry looked down at his father's letter, then met his friend's clueless gaze.

"Next week," he muttered, then crumpled it up in mild anger and tossed it into the hearth.

Henry was only fourteen, but he fancied himself in love.

Madeleine continued the sprightly, happy young woman she had been since their first meeting, laughing and smiling at every opportunity. It was sometimes hard to believe that she was, in fact, faint of heart.

But in the last few weeks, Henry had come to notice the subtle underlying symptoms that she tried to hide, the tiredness that would often catch her off guard. He noticed she would sometimes retire to her chambers in the middle of the day, to regain her strength, Henry assumed, and he would find himself obsessing over news of her reemergence. It always came, the update that she was returned to her former, mischievous self, and before long, Madeleine would be out and about, intent on filling each moment with whatever beauty life had to offer.

It was after one of these bouts of recuperation, just two days before Henry's scheduled and fateful return to England, that he decided he had to make his feelings known before it was too late. For if he would be made to marry another at his father's bidding, he would at least take control over this one matter, lest he regret it for the rest of his life.

"Princess," he said in greeting as he stood before her, having found her enjoying the last of the summer sunshine in the gardens with her ladies.

She looked up, a hand shading her eyes though Henry stood between her and the setting sun. He hoped she would notice the small gesture.

"Prince Henry," she said, and a bubble of pride burst in his chest, as it always did when he was addressed as such. His heart ached suddenly to realise he would not only miss Madeleine upon his leave, but also the way he was so easily accepted by France and its people.

"What brings you here?" she asked, smiling up at him.

Henry opened his mouth but was all of a sudden lost for words. He closed it again. Frowned.

The three ladies surrounding the princess began to giggle, and Henry felt his cheeks redden.

"I was curious to know if you would enjoy a stroll?" he spluttered out then, "With me. Now. *S'il vous plait?*"

"Forward," one girl noted with a playful smirk.

"To the point," another corrected with a nod of approval.

Madeleine, now thirteen and beginning to blossom into womanhood, grinned up at him, "Certainly," and she scrambled up from the blanket on the lawn and wiped down her skirts, "Shall we?"

She presented her arm, and Henry looped it through his, her hand nestled in the crook of his elbow.

The girls began to follow then, which Henry had not minded for he had wanted but a moment with Madeleine, no matter how. But the princess had turned and ordered the girls to stay behind, which both panicked and relieved Henry all at once.

They strolled casually along the edge of the lawn and headed toward the hedgerows that contained a splendid garden within. Henry had often gone there during his leisure time to read the bible by the fountain, or simply to regard the budding roses each morning. As they approached, the sound of the fountain splashing in continuum grew, as if to make clear they had reached their destination.

"You depart soon," Princess Madeleine said matter-of-factly.

Henry nodded, "Much to my dismay."

He tried a chuckle, but it sounded flat even to his ears.

Madeleine smiled, though her gaze remained fixed ahead of her. She examined the beautifully sculpted hedge, a coiled shape reaching seven feet tall.

"I will miss it here," Henry admitted, following her scrutiny of the plant, then looked around himself at the many other splendours.

They took a lap of the garden, a slow wander past the waist-high maze and back to the fountain, where Madeleine sat down at the edge and leaned in to touch the clear water.

"Was there anything in particular you wished to say to me?" she asked then, her grey eyes looking at him without blinking. A challenge in her stare to speak plain and to speak true, for they had but a little time.

Henry looked away, his cheeks burning hot at her directness, and he tentatively sat down beside her.

A hundred things spiralled inside Henry's mind, a thousand different words he could say to gentlemanly express his admiration. But as soon as he'd settled on one sentence or another, the words held suddenly no meaning. At least, no meaning deserving enough to convey how he regarded her as the most wonderful girl he had ever known.

She was looking at him, quietly assessing him as the tips of her fingers continued to glide over the cool water at their side. She smiled faintly at him, a smile that put him both at ease and spurred him on to be brave enough to spill his truth. But no words would do his feelings justice, and before he could stop himself, he leaned forward and pressed his lips to hers.

Her mouth felt soft against his, and he immediately sensed a smile tugging at her lips as he continued to simply press against them. This close, he could smell her scent of honey and lavender, and he pondered if perhaps she had eaten bread and honey for her breakfast. It would certainly explain why she tasted so sweet.

Fireworks erupted in Henry's mind to note she had not pulled away in the split second they had been kissing, but rather, that she was pushing back into him as she too engaged in the kiss, the gentle pressure of her willingness melting away any residual fears he'd had of rejection.

After a moment, Henry pulled away and opened his eyes, a goofy grin on his face conveying his glee, "I apologize for taking the liberty of kissing you," he said, the words tumbling out of him as his subconscious reminded him of his worthlessness.

But Madeleine smiled, then breathed a little laugh, "You ought only to apologise that it took you so long to do it."

September 1533
Hampton Court Palace, London

It was the only joy they would share, for Henry Fitzroy and his household set sail across the channel and arrived back on English soil to the wonderous news that the new queen had given birth.

And the update swept the young man into a whirlpool of worries, completely overshadowing his bruised heart.

Take heed, my son.
Your father has achieved another living child. You'd do well to be ecstatic to behold it.

Henry's stomach lurched at the information brought to him on a hastily scrawled note from his mother.

He frowned. If the child ought to be his replacement as the King of England's beloved son, Henry would hardly be able to contain the disdain on his face if confronted with it.

But he need not have worried, for upon his arrival at the English court in London, he could tell by the atmosphere alone that it was not a desirable outcome.

He looked up at the turrets of the palace, observed each window in search of someone who would clue him in on the developments. As he swung himself off his gelding, he was greeted by a sudden fanfare and his father-in-law, Thomas Howard Duke of Norfolk, emerged from the palace gates.

"Welcome back, Lord Richmond," he said, and Henry felt the pinch at his sudden drop in value, for just hours earlier in France he had been called a prince.

The Duke of Norfolk turned to his son, "Hal!" and clapped him on the back, "You have grown strong! You both have! French customs must have suited you."

Hal, at sixteen, was almost of equal height to his tall father, and yet he bowed his head to receive his favour, "Indeed, Lord Father. The food and wine were of excellent quality."

Then Hal leaned into Henry as his father turned back around and nudged him with his elbow, "And the ladies, right?"

Henry shot him a sideways glance to show he was in no mood for jesting.

"What of my father?" Henry asked Howard now as they made their way inside, "Where is he? Would he not greet his son?"

Norfolk, with his fine, fur-trimmed robes swishing as he went, looked over his shoulder to his ward, "The king is in his chambers. He is busy ordering alterations of the celebrations and announcements following the birth of the princess."

The princess?

There it was: the reason for the gloomy atmosphere.

Henry pressed his lips together tightly, in order to keep himself from showcasing the delight he felt at the information.

A girl was no threat to him. And especially not one who most of the country would deem illegitimate anyway, since she was born within a marriage that was not sanctioned by the pope.

This was good news for Henry, for with this worthless child, he may yet have a chance to be named the king's heir. And with that honour, Henry would surely be able to choose his bride for himself.

King Henry VIII's disappointment in the birth of just another daughter did not last long, for a live child at Anne Boleyn's first attempt was more than Katherine of Aragon had ever achieved, for she had had three stillbirths and only one live birth – a boy which had lived but 52 days – before finally granting him their surviving daughter Mary nine years after their union.

By contrast, Anne Boleyn had proven herself able to maintain a healthy pregnancy throughout, followed by a successful birth, at her very first effort.

Yes, the child was a girl this time, but chances were that the boy she had promised would follow.

And until then, King Henry's plan to secure Anne's status as queen continued.

They named their daughter Elizabeth, in honour of Anne's mother Elizabeth Boleyn and King Henry's late mother Elizabeth of York. Princess Elizabeth went on to receive a grand christening three days after her birth in a ceremony much grander than that of Henry Fitzroy's.

Though they had both, Henry thought, been born out of wedlock.

But young Henry understood the reason for the façade, having learned from his father over the years that the people would accept most anything if it was presented to them well enough. After all, was he not the physical proof of just that?

His father always had been a master of artifice, Henry mused, his many years masquerading as Robin Hood and taking part in masked plays having shown the king that even when the truth was plain to see, the people would believe what their monarch told them. And only few would dare to question it.

But not Henry. He would never openly question anything his father would do, for his future depended wholly on the king's love for him. A love which, Henry had begun to suspect over the years, stemmed less from genuine affection and more from utter desperation.

But before he would be made to marry a girl he did not care for, Henry would presume to confront his father. For surely, he would listen to reason once he was posed with a better option for his only son.

"Lord Father," the young man said some days after his arrival, bowing his head at his king.

King Henry was sitting by the fire in his chambers, a book cracked open on the table before him. He sat up and stretched his arms over his head at his son's entry.

"Come in, son," he said, not yet looking at him. And the young man felt a pinch of uncertainty at the cold reception upon his return. He had been back at the English court for four days, and this was the first time he and his father had shared a private word.

Henry did as he was bid and sat down opposite his father.

The two sat in silence for a while, son watching father as he continued to peruse the book. Henry tried to see what book it was but failed to identify it.

"What brings you here?" the king said then, breaking the silence just as the fire in the hearth spat out an ember. A servant scurried over and flicked the offending fragment back onto the stone fireplace with the welt of his boot.

Henry inhaled to steel himself, knowing his proposition would be the first he had ever dared to bring to his king that would counter his own mandate. He brushed his hand through his auburn curls, so much like his father's.

"It is about my marriage," he said boldly, surprised even by his own forwardness but ultimately unable to beat around the bush.

The king nodded his head as though this conversation had been predicted in the stars, "Splendid, is it not?" he asked, without a hint of frivolity, and without yet looking up.

Henry cleared his throat, crossed his legs, "Well, Father," he said slowly, "I believe it is not in mine – and therefore your – best interest."

At that, the king finally met Henry's gaze. He sagged in his seat and sighed, as though bored to be questioned by his son. But Henry could feel himself being assessed.

He sat up that little bit straighter.

"I mean only that marrying into the Howard family is not our only option," Henry went on, hoping he sounded mature and sagacious, rather than juvenile and eager.

The king narrowed his eyes at his son then, a smirk growing slowly across his face, "Did you have an encounter during your time in France?"

Henry blushed, hating the insinuation in his father's tone that he had acted untoward with Madeleine. The thought alone clenched his stomach.

"No, Father."

"Oh," Henry VIII sat forward in his seat and closed the book, Henry noticing its title then: *The Obedience of a Christian Man*.

"Then what?" the king asked.

Henry frowned, unsure how to word the news he wished to so desperately share. For though he had compiled a solid speech on the ship returning to England, his mind was suddenly scrambled as he sat before his mighty king.

Could he really suggest an alternative proposal to that of his father? Would he be making himself out to be a fool to even believe himself worthy of a Princess of Valois?

"I – I believe that I have been blessed to have gained th – the Princess Madeleine's favour," he stammered then, unable to retreat without voicing his hope. He looked up to meet the king's gaze, "She and I, we share a liking for one another. And if you would permit it, I would be honoured if you would propose our union to King Francis I."

A silence ensued. One in which the king stared back at his son in a way which Henry had never known before.

In his eyes, he saw no longer the twinkle of opportunity as his mind raced to consider all the possibilities he had to elevate his son, but rather a newfound hardness that made Henry want to shrink away.

Had he overstepped? Had his time in France gone to his head and caused him to see in himself something that wasn't there?

Surely not. This was indeed good news. A match between England and France had long been desired by his father. And a royal union for his bastard son had long been prayed for.

"This union would elevate me higher still –" Henry continued, certain his father would wish for the same thing as he.

But then King Henry cut him short with a raise of his hand.

"Enough," he said, with not even a tinge of enthusiasm, "The idea is ludicrous. Why would Francis I accept you for his daughter, a Princess of Valois?"

Henry frowned, bruised by his father's hurtful remark, as well as confused by his change in tune.

"Did you not consider me acceptable to the Princess of Portugal? And Catherine de Medici?"

Henry gathered the book before him, unable to look his son in the eye, "That was then."

Henry blinked, stunned into incredulity, "I must admit, I do not understand. What has changed?"

His father did not answer, rising from his seat instead and heading toward the window where only darkness brewed outside.

What had changed? Henry asked himself as he raced through his memories of what he could have done to irk his father so.

But nothing came to mind. After all, he'd been away in France for nearly a year, doing his father's bidding!

He stood up from his own seat, "Please, Lord Father," he said, "My king...help me comprehend what I have –"

"It is not for you to comprehend, boy!" his father shouted then, causing Henry to flinch, "You do as you are told to, as you have always done, and be a good little boy while you do it. Do I make myself clear!?"

Henry stared at his father in surprise, his blue eyes wide as he looked back into the face so much like his own. He had inherited his father's nose, his eye shape and colour, his hair, even the weakness of his chin. And now, as the moon spilled in through the window where he stood, silvering the king's hair and deepening the bitter lines that bracketed his mouth, Henry saw his own future.

It was one he did not wish for himself.

"Yes," the boy mumbled, though he understood nothing at all. And he hurried out the door.

King Henry feared he had created a monster.

Like his own father before him had done in the later years of his reign, Henry VIII had more recently begun to look at his son in a different light.

It was his letter from France which had alerted him to this dilemma. The one in which he had shared that the French court referred to him as 'Prince Henry'.

This development was something the King of England had worked years to achieve – to have his son be accepted as his potential heir. He had never considered how it may one day come back to haunt him.

Henry hadn't even realised it himself, the threat his son's popularity now posed to his reign. Had it not been for his new wife's remark, warning him how such support from Catholic France could amount to something dangerous, the king might never have seen it, so blinded was he by the love he bore his only son.

But then, it wouldn't have been much of a problem had Queen Anne gone on to give birth to a boy, and not a girl…

But nevertheless, his bastard son's acceptance had become an issue the king could not ignore. After all, Henry VIII had denounced papal authority. All of Catholic Europe was displeased with him and disturbed by his methods; and it would be much more suitable for them if a more malleable young man sat on the throne of England, rather than one who'd had his eyes opened to the pope's control over Europe's monarchs.

And he *finally* understood his father Henry Tudor's paranoia.

"You fear his growing support?" his friend Charles Brandon now asked after the king had hastily explained his concerns to him, following his son's return, "Henry, he is a bastard."

"A bastard I rose high enough precisely to stand a chance of inheritance. He has gained favour from the people over the years and now receives acceptance from Catholic France," the king replied, "A bastard who some would say has a better claim to the throne than the Princess Elizabeth."

Charles had heard the whispers that continued to linger regarding the legality of the king's marriage to Anne Boleyn. He himself agreed with them. But Charles had known Henry long enough to realise when he needed calming. And this was one of those times.

"Your son is loyal to you," he assured, "Even if he *did* have enough support to gather an army, which I highly doubt he could, he would not. He loves Your Majesty. And he was not born into a race for the throne. I can guarantee he has not once considered usurpation."

"So you think it, too?!" Henry replied suddenly, his eyes wild.

"Henry?"

"You said the word yourself: usurpation. You came to that conclusion yourself."

Charles frowned, "I am telling you that I do *not* believe him to be capable of it or even willing."

The king sucked air in through his yellowing teeth and shook his head, "I am not so sure anymore, Charles. The boy wished for me to ask King Francis I for his daughter Madeleine's hand in marriage. I denied him it."

Charles shrugged, "There you have it then. He shall marry the Howard girl and lose all hope of gaining any support through marriage."

"But what of the public?"

"What of them?"

King Henry raked his fingers through his hair, "They continue displeased with Queen Anne."

The side of Charles' mouth twitched, he also did not think highly of the lady, but he would not ever voice his thoughts to his king. He had seen too many other men fall for having been honest with the king about their personal beliefs.

"Let them grumble," he said instead, "You are the king *and* Supreme Head of the Church of England. You had Anne crowned with St Edward's crown itself. She is your rightful queen and Princess Elizabeth your heir presumptive, until a boy is born by Anne. And then, once you have that boy, they shall have nothing more to say."

November 1533

Although King Henry had delivered the news and made the arrangements, it was actually Queen Anne who had suggested the match between Henry Fitzroy and her kinswoman Mary Howard. Even before her husband had begun to worry about his bastard son's growing approval from the people, she had long seen him – as well as the Princess Mary – as a threat.

There was danger in the king's love for his son, and though Anne Boleyn had not initially wanted this life for herself, now that she had her own child to consider, she would not think twice about infringing on someone else's stability in order to secure her daughter's future.

In the years prior to Anne's ascendancy, who Henry Fitzroy would marry had been a non-issue for Anne, but now that she was queen, a marriage such as to a foreign princess would be a threat to Anne's status. For it would place Fitzroy in a strong position as a rival claimant to the throne of England against any of her own children.

It was perturbing to consider how, not long ago, there had been many discussions around naming Fitzroy as the king's heir – just as there had been discussions in the past around naming his daughter by Katherine of Aragon as his heir. For as a woman who knew she had many enemies at court who would prefer Fitzroy to any of her children to take the throne, Anne believed therefore that her position as queen and her children's positions as successors relied solely on the besmirchment of the king's other children.

And so, marrying Henry Fitzroy to her cousin Mary Howard, not only contained the boy's potential to gain a more advantageous marriage, but it also further solidified the idea that her kin was worthy of being members of the royal family.

"He will marry your cousin, as agreed," King Henry assured her one evening, after she had, as casually as she could, broached the subject yet again.

She sighed with relief and smiled up at her husband, "It is for the best," she purred, "The boy was brought up a Catholic. He cannot be allowed to form a Catholic bond with a royal princess, no less."

"I said he will marry the Howard girl," King Henry interrupted, "I have heard your reasoning before, and I agree. I had not considered it back then, but, in hindsight, leaving him behind to form relationships in a Catholic country which we have always had a rivalry with was not my finest moment. Not when I have made my decision abundantly clear that it shall be sons by *you* that will take precedence in the line of succession."

Anne leaned forward and placed her small hand on his forearm, "It is only natural that you would leave your bastard son behind to gather information from the French. How were you to know that he would come back with ideas in his head?"

The king's mouth twitched, and he pulled his arm away, "You think he has considered it?"

Anne Boleyn blinked, ever since she had planted the seed of doubt in her husband's head, it appeared to have sprouted significantly, and quite without watering.

"I think," she said slowly, running her fingers up and down his arm, "That you and I ought to take to bed and attempt to create a son who will do his father proud."

The king looked down at her hand on him, then back up at her, the great lust of his life, and grinned.

"I say, wife, that is a spectacular idea."

Chapter 15

Is it wrong that I write to you at a time like this, Prince Henry?
I hope you do not think so, for I have wanted to write to you ever since you left.
Was it but two months ago? It feels as though it has been years, your absence dragging my days into an unrelenting slog.
I know you are to marry. I know it is to be soon. News like that does not stay secret for very long.
With that knowledge I feel a little foolish to even be writing this. But I thought it important that you know, so that we may both close that short but sweet chapter in our lives: If I had the luxury of choice, it would have been you. If I were but a pauper, or you a true-born prince, it may have been so. But alas, the stars were not aligned for us. And for that there must have been a reason.
Nevertheless, I will cherish that little flame that had flickered between us, despite having to now snuff it out. For we each have our paths to tread, and I am likely not long for this world anyhow.
I say this only to alleviate whatever guilt or wishful thinking that may be lingering within you, Henry, so that you may enter the union with this other lady and be free to nurture whatever may grow. I hope something wonderful takes root for you there. You deserve nothing but happiness, for you are good. As good as can be.
I shall always miss you, Henry. But let us not dwell on something that never had a chance to survive to begin with.
I wish you all the love, though it be not mine.

Yours – but no longer – Princess Madeleine of Valois

26th November 1533
Hampton Court Palace

In a discreet and private ceremony – attended only by young Henry's mother, his sister, the Duke of Norfolk and his wife Elizabeth Howard – Mary Howard, a girl of fourteen, was trembling beside Henry Fitzroy as the priest mumbled on.

Hidden behind a white veil, Henry couldn't make out her features, but he had noted that she had reddish hair that fell to her lower back in waves.

She was short and skinny for her age, appearing no more than twelve years old at first glance. And Henry, who at fourteen already stood at five feet eight inches tall, couldn't help but wonder, yet again, why they had been matched.

My cousin the queen is behind it, his friend Hal had informed him some days earlier, Hal's loyalty seeming like a pendulum that swayed back and forth between his friend and his cousin Anne Boleyn. Of course, this new wife of Henry's was also Queen Anne's cousin. And Henry wondered exactly where *her* loyalties would lie.

His fists clenched and unclenched at his sides at the thought of the woman who was actively trying to ruin his chances of ever becoming king. And he realised then, that even though the former Queen of England had made her distaste of his existence clear, and had made him feel uncomfortable throughout the years, at least she had never dared to interfere in his future.

Anne Boleyn's reasons were easy enough to understand. For she was acting in the best interest of *her* child. But why his father would agree to this lesser marriage for his only son was something that remained unanswered. Henry could not fathom it.

He opened his hands and wiped his palms on his trousers upon noticing their tight grip. He needed to remain calm.

He needed to figure this out.

For years King Henry VIII had been trying to elevate his son as high as he possibly could, laying titles upon titles at his feet. Responsibilities, important connections, knowledge, the public's attention – and all for what?

Had Henry failed his father somehow that he now deserved this punishment? Had he lost his worth when he came home from France with little to no valuable information?

Or was it quite the opposite entirely?

Henry exhaled out his nose in frustration. Frustration at not knowing. Frustration at his lack of control over his own goddamned life!

The girl beside him raised her head and cast a quick glance in his direction then, as though she could sense his exasperation. Or maybe she had simply heard his angry exhale.

He turned briefly towards her, and though he could not see her features properly, glancing at the veiled form only reminded Henry of the girl he would rather have seen next him on this occasion.

The corners of his mouth dropped at the thought of Madeleine's letter, releasing him from whatever it had been between them, as if it was that easy to simply turn off how he felt. He looked away, anger beginning to bubble inside him again when suddenly, he realised something.

On the cushion beneath the girl's knees where they both knelt before the mumbling priest, Henry had noticed dark little splotches in the fabric, as if wetted by something. Or someone. He returned his attention forward, troubled by his self-centred thoughts.

This was not just happening to him. She, too, very clearly did not want to be here.

It is a man's world. And we women are but allowed to live in it.

She, too, had not asked for this. And if her trembling hands and hastened breathing was not proof enough, the teardrops staining the cushion said it all.

He softened towards her then, realising they were both in the same boat. With a sigh, Henry reshuffled his thoughts, choosing to focus on the positives.

Despite not knowing her or choosing her, he would make the best of this marriage. There must be something they would find that they had in common. After all, she was his best friend's sister. That should count for something, at least.

Enter the union with this other lady and be free to nurture whatever may grow. I hope something wonderful takes root for you there.

The girl was not to blame, Henry knew, for she was not the orchestrator of her life. No young girls – or bastard sons – ever were.

With his new mindset, Henry reached across what had previously felt like an enormous gulf between them and took her delicate hand in his. He heard her gasp at his unexpected touch, and he cast a tentative glance in her direction, hoping to convey some comfort, some reassurance.

Even with her head turned to face him, Henry still did not have a lucid view through the veil. But he continued to look at her anyway, as though his new perspective would somehow allow him to see her more clearly.

Due to their young age, the new couple was instructed not to consummate their marriage, and to wait until both parties were at least within their sixteenth year – much to their relief.

They spent their wedding night on opposite sides of the four-poster bed instead, the pair with their backs turned towards the other, warding off any unwanted conversation.

Henry lay there, still and quiet, his eyes darting around his side of the room while the minutes flew by. Hours must have passed, for the roaring fire in their hearth had died down to pulsating embers. And yet sleep would not find him. His mind was too uneasy, too filled with could-have-beens.

"Are you asleep?" came a whispered voice suddenly, jolting him in surprise.

He turned to the sound, looking over his shoulder.

His young wife had turned towards him, her hands pressed together as if in prayer between her cheek and the pillow as she looked at him from across the mattress with shining eyes.

He turned around to face her, "Haven't slept a wink," he admitted, realising it was the first thing he had said to her.

Mary Howard blinked, "Me neither."

They smiled at each other awkwardly then. And Henry took the opportunity to really look at her.

She had long reddish-brown hair and equally coloured eyebrows above green, heavily lidded eyes. In the darkness they appeared the colour of the woods at twilight, and Henry found himself wondering what their true green would be once he was able to look at her at daybreak. He continued to peruse her, to assess the outer shell of the person his soul was now bound to for life. Her skin was extremely pale, so much so he thought he could see blue veins across her chest –

"Did you want to –?" she asked suddenly, noticing his examination of her.

Henry frowned at her in the darkness, "What?"

She opened her mouth, then closed it, and Henry noticed her top lip was thin, while her bottom lip was plumper.

The side of his mouth twitched to think of Madeleine, and their departing kiss.

Mary exhaled in a way which made Henry think she was stilling herself, and he remained silent, giving her time.

"Did you want to – you know?" and she lay onto her back, her eyes continuing fixed on him as she did so.

Henry, realising then what she was asking, cleared his throat uncomfortably.

"Oh, no," he said, "We were advised not to."

"I know," Mary admitted, glancing away then, "But if you wanted to, you would be within your rights."

"I don't want to."

Mary nodded once, "I only needed to make sure. After all, you are my husband now."

Henry swallowed and sat up, his nightcap feeling suddenly tight. He shook his head.

"You need not fret about that," Henry said, hoping to assure her.

Mary frowned, and Henry noticed the confusion in her expression.

"I love another," he blurted out then, the truth falling out of him like a gift he could no longer hide.

At that, Mary sat up and smiled at him, her long wavy hair like a murky river over her shoulder.

"You do?" she asked, her voice having grown giddy, as though she and Henry had just become friends, "Who is she?"

Henry breathed a stunned laugh. It was quite the opposite reaction he had imagined from his wife to the news that he had feelings for someone else.

"You do not know her," he said, embarrassed for a moment, "She is not at English court."

"At French court then," Mary said, scooting forward as if she were gossiping with her ladies.

Henry did not answer, opting for subtlety, "It does not matter. She and I were not to be," and he lay back down.

Mary was nodding sombrely as he looked up at her, still sitting up in the middle of the bed.

She sighed heavily then, like some heavy reality had just hit her.

She lay down slowly on her back, arranging her long hair out from underneath her, and looking up at the panelled ceiling. Then she turned her head to look at her new husband, the two of them laying closer together.

"God help us all if not even the son of the king can get what he wants."

February 1534

In the months that followed, Henry thought of Madeleine often, and how different he may have felt about the concept of marriage had it been she who had met him at the altar.

It no longer mattered, however, for what was done was done. And if word was to be believed, Madeleine's health continued fragile over in France. It was probably for the best that he had not succeeded in his quest to marry her, for the English climate may very well have been the death of her. This was what he would tell himself at night when his dreams would take him back to the luscious gardens of Château Amboise, and he would wake to find the memory dispersing from his mind's eye like fog. Some mornings, the scent of the marguerites and clover that had been in bloom that day by the fountain would linger in his nostrils, and he would be transported back to their private moment. The instant in which he had braved his fears and dared the world to remind him of his worthlessness. But instead, Madeleine had accepted him, for all his unimportance.

It made him resent his father then, who he understood was the true cause of all his troubles – even above the queen who put forward the idea that he should marry Mary Howard – for it was the king who ultimately called the shots.

But Henry shook his head. It did him no good to get tangled up in resentment. All it would do was make him bitter and hateful, and he did not wish to become like that. Like his father.

For most of his life, Henry had looked at his father and seen the most majestic and benevolent king to ever have lived. He had, many nights throughout his childhood, prayed that he would one day grow up to become even half as grand as King Henry VIII. But as the years had gone by, the young man had learned things that he did not like: that beneath the extravagant and charismatic exterior was a man whose values and morals were deeply misplaced. The king was inherently angry, paranoid and desperate.

And those were not qualities Henry wished to shape himself after.

If Henry were to take inspiration from someone, to mould himself from a boy into a man, he had decided that his father would not be his muse. It may have been, a long time ago when Henry was yet too young and blinded by his gifts and promises to see his true colours.

But, in his most recent bout of wisdom, Henry wished only to be like one man in his life.

The man who had taught him far more about being a man than the king's tutors ever could: his always loved and sorely missed stepfather, Gilbert Tailboys.

April 1534

The previous month, Parliament had finally passed the Act of Supremacy – which categorically defined Henry VIII as Supreme Head of the Church of England – as well as the Act of Succession – which secured the succession of the children of Henry VIII by Anne Boleyn and excluded the former Princess Mary, now demoted to Lady Mary, from inheriting the throne of England.

Queen Katherine was henceforth to be referred to as Dowager Princess of Wales, and the whole nation had to swear an oath that they accepted these Acts as law.

It was a tense time within England. There were not many who were brave enough to stand firm in their beliefs and reject the king's oath, and there would be fewer still once Henry VIII turned against his own friend and former Lord Chancellor, Thomas More.

To reject the oath is treason! Thomas Cromwell, Henry VIII's newly appointed Chief Minister, had argued as he'd banged his fist upon the table, the other members of the council watching in silent awe.

Then I shall have to commit treason! Thomas More had replied hotly, having been summoned before the council, *For there is no amount of threat and pressure you or anyone may force upon me which would make me condemn my soul for the love of an earthly king! No king is Supreme Head of a Church above the Pope!*

And so it was that Thomas More, who had once – like Wolsey – been so cordial with the king, was arrested for treason against the crown.

Bishop John Fisher, who had been a Tudor supporter for decades and close personal friend to Henry VIII's own beloved grandmother Margaret Beaufort, was also arrested shortly thereafter.

But most frightening still, was the swift execution of the Nun of Kent Elizabeth Barton, who had been found guilty of preaching against the king's new marriage, and been hanged for her treason.

It seemed no one was safe, and Henry Fitzroy feared for his half-sister, who, according to court gossip, had also refused to sign the oath.

"She is holding firm in her belief that her mother is the rightful queen," Hal informed Henry as they returned from their hunt one afternoon, servants travelling behind them pushing carts with two dead boars strapped to them.

Henry inhaled and looked carefully over his shoulder, "Of course she does," he whispered back, "she seeks to maintain her legitimacy. It is not something I would throw away either."

Hal sighed, "Whether she signs or not, her legitimacy is void with the king's annulment."

Henry nodded pensively.

"We have signed the oath of course," Hal added.

"As have my mother, my siblings and I," Henry replied, "It is too dangerous not to."

Hal cleared his throat nervously, aware of what his friend was referring to. For along with those two new acts, the king had passed another law which truly highlighted his paranoia to all who had previously but assumed it.

"How does it even work?" Hal asked in a hushed voice, stopping his gelding at the sound of the cart's wheel getting stuck. The two young men turned to observe as their guards helped the servants haul the wooden cart out of the rut, groaning at its load with the boar's dead weight on top.

"As far as I understand, you need but mention it and it is regarded treason," Henry replied in an equally lulled tone.

It, the topic the king had deemed illegal and treasonous to even broach: his death.

"Surely even to discuss the succession, then, is treason," Hal countered logically, turning his horse around once the men had hauled the cart out of the groove.

Henry raised his pale eyebrows at his friend in agreement, hoping that to say nothing further would encourage Hal to do the same. For Henry was all too aware of his father's perplexing avoidance of him of late, causing him to fear that perhaps the king's love for his son was a thing of the past.

And it made Henry Fitzroy feel suddenly vulnerable in a way that was completely foreign to him.

"To pass a law to control the people's thoughts and casual conversations," Hal added brazenly, causing Henry to hastily look over his shoulder for fear of being overhead, "it could cause neighbour to turn against neighbour. And it might very well even lead to innocent people being put to death for a misunderstanding."

Henry cleared his throat, "I shall speak of it no further. You know of my standing on this. It isn't right. But I am not foolish enough to further fuel this conversation."

And with that he urged his gelding into a trot, putting distance between him and the last remnants of an exchange which, if found out, could very well cost him his head.

May 1534

The king was in high spirits, for the queen was with child once again.

Henry VIII was so overjoyed that he walked throughout the palace with a straight back and his head held high, stretching out his full 6ft 2" frame. He ordered a silver cradle be made for his new child, who he of course believed – and prayed – would be a boy. He went all out, ordering the cradle to be decorated with precious stones and have the Tudor rose etched onto it.

It was a sure sign to the court that he had enough faith in his new wife that he would warrant spending so much on the child before it was even born, or before the queen was even showing. It also demonstrated to the world that he was certain Anne Boleyn would not fail him as Katherine of Aragon had.

By the way he was flaunting Queen Anne's pregnancy about, it would seem his worries about pregnancies ending in miscarriage were a thing of the past.

And so, it came as a huge blow to the king and court when his queen woke up one morning with terrible cramping and bloodied sheets.

"The baby comes too soon," the midwife hissed at another as she sent her away to fetch warm water and clean cloths.

"What is happening?" Anne Boleyn cried, holding one hand over her slightly rounded belly as it contracted in pain.

The midwife did not reply and instead hurried about the queen's chambers like an angered wasp, flitting to-and-fro to ready the queen for what would undoubtedly be the worst day of her life.

Chapter 16

1535

There was much unrest throughout the country, almost as if the king was taking out his frustrations on the nation.

More people were being arrested for refusing to sign the Oath of Supremacy, men including John Houghton, Prior of London Charter House, and Richard Reynolds. Both men were hung, drawn and quartered at Tyburn.

Thomas More and Bishop Fisher, who the public knew to be loyal and respectable men, had continued imprisoned in the Tower of London for over a year. And now the order for their execution was passed, both having been condemned as traitors to the crown for failing to accept the king as the Supreme Head of the Church of England. Their punishment, like the others before them, was to be hung, drawn and quartered. But King Henry VIII, hoping to be viewed as forgiving, had allowed them to receive a swifter death at the last moment, and ruled that they be beheaded instead.

Many others met their end for their unwillingness to bow to the king's warped will, spurring those who were previously unsure in their decision to submit or expect to die for their beliefs.

Henry Fitzroy knew of the people's fears, could feel it in the air as though it were a physical thing as he attended the executions of those who would deny their king.

Henry had attended Thomas More's beheading – much to the young man's dismay – for as a member of the royal family and the king's only son, he had been selected to act as the monarch's representative at these religious persecutions. His presence indicating to the world that the King of England approved of the horrific events.

Three Carthusian monks were to die on this day, another public execution Henry had been made to attend in his father's stead; and he steeled himself for what horror he knew was to come.

For these poor fellows would not be as fortunate as Fisher or More.

As his father's representative, Henry knew not to show the crowd his true emotions, and to keep his face clear of any consternation. But underneath his mask of neutrality, Henry was appalled and, quite frankly, alarmed by King Henry's actions.

Henry's stomach churned now to see the men – the convicted traitors – arriving at the gallows fastened to a wooden panel drawn by a horse, their skin ripped away at the ankles and calves, a trail of blood dragging behind them as they moaned in pain.

They were then hanged almost to the point of death, their bodies twitching and squirming, urine trickling down their legs as they choked and spluttered. Henry had to swallow hard to avoid gagging at the horrific scene. They were then cut down moments before death and beheaded; and Henry breathed a sigh of relief that their pain was finally over. But as if that wasn't enough, their bodies were then quartered for good measure.

All the while, Henry did not look away – though the acid had been rising in his throat. He had not dared to, for fear that his abhorrence for the king's actions would be found out.

And he wondered, not for the first time, just how far his father was willing to go in his crazed pursuit of a 'suitable' male heir. Especially when he already had one right under his nose.

June 1535
Kenninghall, Norfolk

"He avoids me still," Henry admitted to his wife, as he peeled off his jacket and hung it on the back of his chair, "He sends me out to represent him, I continue invited to banquets and Parliament and events, but he and I nevermore meet like we once did."

They were settling down for a private dinner at the Howard residence of Kenninghall in Norfolk, Mary and Henry having agreed after their marriage that though they were to live apart until they were older, they would convene away from court once per month, in order to get to know each other better.

Henry and Mary had grown to respect one another since their forced union nearly two years prior, the young man and woman having learned much about each other that they found agreeable.

Henry had been right. As the sister of his best friend, Mary shared many similarities to Hal that he enjoyed. Her quick humour and sharp mind aside, she was someone who listened intently and always tried to offer solutions, despite the fact that her loyalties – like Hal's – most likely lay with their cousin Anne Boleyn. Although Henry had considered of late how, of all people, surely she ought to wish for her husband to succeed. After all, she would become the next Queen of England if he did.

And yet he did not dare ever ask where she stood, yet unable to gauge whether she was completely trustworthy.

"Did you and the king not go hunting together last week?" Mary asked as she perused the food before her, "My Lord Father mentioned something about that, I think."

Henry sipped his wine, "We did, but that hardly led to much interaction."

Mary frowned slightly, "And you continue in the dark as to the king's reason for all this? I mean, you *are* his only son. Surely –"

"I am well aware I am his only son," Henry interrupted, "That is precisely why his sudden rejection of me is so baffling."

Mary ate some roasted pork and chewed pensively.

"Perhaps that is precisely it," she said after a moment.

Henry looked up from his own plate, "What is?"

"That you are his only son."

The young man made a face, urging her to be clear.

Mary wiped the corners of her mouth with her handkerchief.

"Think about it," she said, "If you have done nothing to irk the king, yet he acts like you have, then the only plausible explanation that is left is that you have not done anything."

"And yet he *is* irked with me," Henry added, in a tone that would suggest she was not making sense.

But Mary only smiled, "Exactly."

Henry shook his head, "There is no logic behind that."

"Of course there is," Mary countered, "If you have not done anything to explain such rejection, then the problem must be with his perception of you. Have you noticed the king acting paranoid towards you? Threatened perhaps?"

At that, Henry froze mid-chew, his eyes raising to lock with hers across the table.

"Threatened, how?" Henry asked, "And why? I have never given him cause to doubt me."

Mary shrugged then and averted her gaze, causing Henry to narrow his eyes at her.

"What do you know?" he asked.

"I don't actually know anything," she admitted, her hands raised in earnest. To his surprise, Henry believed her, "But my Lady Mother and Queen Anne had something of a falling out, if you recall?"

He did. Mary's mother, Elizabeth Howard – having been rather against her daughter's marriage to the king's bastard son – had caused quite the scene, scolding the new queen – her own niece – for her interference in Mary's future.

"I remember," Henry pressed.

"Well," Mary continued, "My mother has since been quite liberal with her opinions of the queen. She has, more than once, expressed her distaste of Queen Anne's methods. And how she puts ideas in the king's head."

She had Henry's full attention, his cutlery at either side of his plate, his food forgotten.

"You think she has put an idea in my father's head? An idea that would incite this fear in him that I am a threat?"

Mary shrugged, "It is but a theory," she admitted, "You yourself have confessed you have done nothing but his bidding, have done nothing to have spurred this bizarre detachment from you."

Henry's eyes remained narrowed as he thought, his mouth hanging slightly open in utter awe of his wife's mind.

It appeared that perhaps she was more in favour of *him* sitting the throne than her cousin, after all.

For what she was saying made complete sense, and he was surprised that he hadn't ever thought of it himself.

Mary grinned, pleased with herself, "You see," she said smugly, popping a piece of roast pork into her mouth, "There's more to me than a pretty face."

And though neither love nor lust had never blossomed between the two, in that moment, Henry could have kissed his wife for her smarts.

It was as if understanding his father's fears had somehow erased them, for not long after Henry and Mary had deduced that it was suspicion that had led the king's behaviour against his son in recent years, his manner towards Henry changed entirely.

But of course, it had nothing to do with Henry's understanding of his father's psyche, but rather the timing of it, for since Queen Anne's miscarriage the year before, the king's obsession with her had begun to fade. And with his love for her dwindling, he began to return his affection towards those he had previously discarded.

For over a year, Anne Boleyn's womb had continued empty month after month, and it was growing increasingly clear to the court that the king was becoming less infatuated with her now that she was proving that perhaps it *wasn't* due to Katherine of Aragon that the king had been unable to sire legitimate sons.

Just last week, the rumour mill had begun turning once again, whispers flying around the palace that Queen Anne had raged at the king for displaying interest in another lady at court.

You must shut your eyes! As your predecessor knew well enough to do!

He had supposedly bellowed, reminding the new queen of how fragile her position really was. That is, if rumours were to be believed.

Since then, however, Henry had noticed that Queen Anne had been a lot less engaging at court events, and a lot less fawned over by the king at banquets and celebrations.

Tension was in the air, there was no doubt about it. And with the queen's influence over the king lessening, he began to show favour to his bastard son once again, only further confirming to Henry that it had indeed been her words of malice that had turned his father against him.

My son shall be sent to Ireland, the king had proclaimed to his council following the subject's lengthy discussion, reviving his plan from several years ago, *To be made King of Ireland.*

The king's council had looked about at one another, still concerned with the idea but too fearful to deny the king at such a time, and, begrudgingly, they'd all nodded their heads.

The glaring coincidence of it all – his potential to rise again now that his father was displeased with the queen – did not escape Henry Fitzroy. And he realised that to be within the king's close circle was as dangerous as it was prosperous.

One just had to know how to sail the stormy sea.

September 1535

"I shall miss you," Henry admitted to his younger sister Elizabeth as he said his goodbyes to his family.

Elizabeth, now fifteen and grown, was a pretty young girl, with hair as bright as their father's, but a smile that was all their mother's. She would soon find a good match, Henry hoped, for she deserved the world. Besides Hal, his sister had always been his best friend.

"You must write to us every day," their mother reminded him as she wiped a tear from her face.

"Of course, Mother," he replied, before his mind returned to the strange turn of events in the past two years.

It had been a dark and gloomy time, ever since he had returned from France with what he had believed to have been good news: his acceptance as a Prince of England by France, and the Princess Madeleine's approval to court her.

It had felt, at the time, like the most splendid stage of his life, where his future had appeared clear and abounding. But when his father had practically flinched in horror at the news, as though Henry had proposed the most atrocious of ideas, the brilliant future he had foreseen had been snuffed out like a candle in a strong wind.

But no more. His father's light shone on him anew. And this time, he would not allow anyone to leave him in shadow ever again.

October 1535
Ludlow Castle, Wales

Henry Fitzroy, his household, and army travelled in stages from London to Ireland, and arrived in Wales to make the crossing.

They made camp at Ludlow Castle in Wales as they were instructed to, to await the king's command before proceeding on their journey.

"King of Ireland," Hal said with a grin that first evening, as he leaned back in his chair and locked his hands behind his head.

His words echoed through the halls of the castle.

The castle was the traditional seat of the Prince of Wales when he was sent to learn how to rule. It was where Edward IV had sent his son in 1473, and where Henry Tudor had sent his heir Prince Arthur.

Henry's father, King Henry VIII, had not presided over the Prince's Council, for he had not been brought up to rule. The last royal to have resided here in preparation of their kingly duties had been the former Princess Mary, Henry's half-sister, before their father had decided she had not been worth it and begun his chase of Anne Boleyn.

It felt like such a long time ago now. Back when Henry had been appointed an Earl and a Duke and Knight of the Garter all in the same month. Back when the king had put his faith in his two surviving children despite the fact that one was a girl, and the other was a bastard. The king had worked with what he'd had and been glad to do so. And yet it had not been enough.

Henry wondered then if his father would still have pursued his mistress so aggressively, whether his 'love' for her would have sustained his cause, if he had known she would fail in procuring him a son, too.

But it no longer mattered, for he was being sent to Ireland to establish himself as its king. He had succeeded, finally, in his quest to be accepted as good enough.

Henry grinned across the table at his friend, "King of Ireland," he repeated smugly, feeling as though he had finally won some kind of unattainable game.

"And my sister to be your queen," Hal added, to which Henry raised his glass.

They waited for instructions from London for two days, Henry growing more anxious with each hour that passed, when finally, he was put out of his misery with the arrival of a messenger.

"What news?" Henry asked the boy.

"King Henry recalls you to return, my lord," the messenger panted, to which Henry flinched, "he says you are needed at Parliament."

Henry clenched his jaw at the outright falsehood with which his father would summon him back, knowing immediately that there would be more to it than that. For surely, attending Parliament was hardly as urgent as his journey to take Ireland.

Like every other time he had been *this close* to achieving his destiny, it was pulled out from underneath him. And really, Henry scolded himself for having believed it all over so easily. But, as ever, the king's son did as he was bid, knowing that to maintain a steady relationship with his father, he ought to never rock the boat.

His party made their return to London, as instructed, the mood glum and silently pensive.

They were three miles outside of Stamford, four hours into their return journey, when another messenger was spotted in the distance, a cloud of dust billowing behind him.

Henry slowed his gelding, his guards and those few hundred behind following suit.

"What now?" he had muttered to himself, narrowing his eyes, as though to see the man approaching with more clarity would somehow give him insight into his father's sporadic thoughts.

Parliament had been cancelled. That was the second messenger's news. And Henry sent him away with nothing but a scowl, though he had known the call to Parliament had been but a ruse to begin with.

The reason as to *why* however, was yet to be guessed.

"Of course," Henry mumbled emotionlessly the following day, having returned to court shortly after daybreak, "Of course she is with child! It is the only plausible explanation. The only reason why my father would choose not to go through with his plan for me. Why grant me Ireland now when a potential *legitimate* male heir may very well be born soon?"

He laughed humourlessly, the coincidence being too great not to.

Mary Howard had met her husband in the courtyard following Henry's return, and informed him of the news.

"She announced it privately to the king the eve of your departure," she told him in a hushed tone, taking heed to maintain neutral in her delivery, for as a lady-in-waiting to her cousin the queen, she felt constantly torn as to her loyalty when it came to sharing information about her with her husband.

At that, Henry scoffed, "Of course she did," he said, "Anything to keep me from rising."

Mary exhaled, she did not like to think of her cousin as that cunning, "She cannot have planned to conceive in time with the king's decision for you. She has no control over when she will be with child. If that were the case, she would have had another baby before now."

Henry's eyebrows twitched, though he knew his wife was right, of course. On this occasion at least, Queen Anne had not *planned* to quash his elevation.

"If this child is a boy –"

He did not need to complete his sentence, for Mary was already nodding, "If it is a boy, you shall lose your place," she sighed, "And yet it is the most desirable outcome."

Henry frowned and took a step away from her, in order to look her in the eyes, "You believe that?" he said, "Even if by my continuing to be the king's only son you would one day become Queen of England, at the very least Queen of Ireland?"

Mary breathed a little laugh at his question, "All this plotting and scheming," she said, shaking her head, "I have no heart for it. Do I sometimes consider how glorious it would be to sit upon the throne as your consort? Of course! The thought has crept into my mind on the odd occasion. I'd be lying if I said it hadn't. But the queen is once again with child, and that is a blessing. Chances are it will be a boy this time. It is what I pray for, even if only to end this constant tug of war between all those reaching for the crown. You, the Lady Mary, Queen Anne," she shook her head, "England needs stability now. And if Queen Anne delivers the king a son, we shall finally know peace again."

Henry swallowed, surprised by her response, for he had believed her to have been rooting for him. But then again, he should be used to people betraying him by now.

"You have made your choice then?" he asked, making sure not to let his emotions be known.

Mary looped her arm with his and sighed, "I have," she admitted, "It is the right thing to do. The king will never fully accept you as his heir, you must know that by now."

Henry flinched, unable to control his body's reaction to her bluntness. He did not retract his arm from hers, however, choosing instead to pretend like he was slowly coming to terms with that possibility.

Chapter 17

January 1536
Windsor Castle, Berkshire

  Henry and his household were back at court and returned to their old routine. The matter of his ascension as King of Ireland was put to bed, not to be broached again until after the queen had delivered her baby. And only then, if the child was another girl, or indeed, born dead.
Despite Henry's disappointment at being withdrawn from his destiny, he was glad to note that his father's paranoia had not returned. Or, if it had, that Henry appeared no longer to be the sole focus or cause of it.
The Christmastide festivities came and went, the court a merry cacophony of sounds.
The queen's pregnancy continued to thrive, her bump already being visible underneath her gowns of gold and royal purple. Gifts were exchanged, the king giving to and receiving from all his favourites in a grand display of wealth and delight – all an extravagant attempt to eradicate the gloom of the preceding few years.
As if 1535 had not been eventful enough, news had come the previous month from the Imperial Ambassador, Eustace Chapuys, that the former queen, Katherine of Aragon, had taken ill. She had sent word to His Majesty – whom she still loved despite all the heartache he had caused her – to allow her to say her goodbyes to their daughter, Mary, whom she had not seen or corresponded with in years, as per the king's orders.
King Henry had pondered the request for several seconds before deciding it was far too great a risk to allow the dying woman to see their child. For though the two women had accepted all he had thrown at them throughout the years, and reduced them to no more than a bastard daughter and a Dowager Princess of Wales, Katherine and Mary still had too

much support from the people. And the king could not risk the chance that they would yet plot against him. Not when he was yet to gain a son from Queen Anne.

And truth be told, the king had not entirely believed the news of her ill health, his suspicious mind choosing to see strategy in everyone's moves. He imagined it far more likely that Katherine was not ill at all, but attempting to pull the wool over his eyes.

It came as somewhat of a surprise then when, just a few weeks later, amidst the cheer and dancing and laughter, news broke that the beloved Katherine of Aragon had died.

Alone, heartbroken, and in pain.

Kyme, Lincolnshire

The country was in mourning for the woman who many still believed in their hearts to have been their queen.

And yet no grand funeral was being arranged for her, no royal procession was being organised for mourners to walk behind.

Instead, Katherine of Aragon was to be quietly buried at St Peterborough Abbey in a few days' time, rather than at the monastery belonging to the Franciscan Observant Friars where she had requested to be buried. The king had ordered for her to receive a service befitting that of a princess, and not of a queen, further reminding the country that he believed her never to have been his lawful wife to begin with.

"She never liked me much," Henry Fitzroy now reflected to his mother with a chuckle, some days after the noble lady's death.

He had gone to visit his mother, sister, and brothers in the home where he had lived until he was six, when he had been plucked from their nucleus and declared potentially important enough to receive a noble education.

He had gone on to receive many duties. But what *really* had he achieved on this path his father had set him on? Had it really been worth it?

His mother had inherited the Kyme estates when Gil Tailboys had died in 1530, and though she had remarried the previous year in 1535 – to a soldier called Edward Fiennes de Clinton, who was twelve years her junior – they had decided to settle at Bessie's Lincolnshire estates instead of his family seat in Kent. Much to Henry's delight, for he loved that country residence more than any grand castle.

His mother seemed happy, the couple appearing very much in love. And it made Henry glad to see her smiling once again, after having remained in widowhood following Gil's passing for almost five years.

Bessie breathed a laugh now and flashed a warm smile at her eldest son, who was just two years younger than she herself had been when she had given birth to him.

"Of course she didn't," she said, "You were the one thing Queen Katherine wished for all her life: a surviving male child. It would have avoided all that has happened. It was never personal."

Henry considered this, then wondered if the new queen's dislike of him was also 'never personal'.

"I suppose so," he said, briefly weighing up the two women his father had chosen for wives.

"She will be missed," Bessie admitted then, as they continued their walk among the gardens.

For January, it was a pleasant enough day, with a clear sky and only a mild breeze.

Henry raised his eyebrows, "Not by everyone," he added, knowing Bessie would know of whom he spoke.

"Ah," his mother replied, extracting her hand from beneath her furs and waving it in the air, "Don't be so sure."

Henry frowned at his mother and turned to search her face, "What do you mean?" he asked.

Bessie inhaled, one pale eyebrow raised, "Queen Anne is in a precarious position now that Katherine is dead."

Henry's eyes narrowed as he failed to understand. A flock of geese flew overhead then, honking to one another to maintain their form.

Bessie looped her arm around her son's and guided them down the two steps leading further into the gardens. Pebbles crunched underfoot.

"It all hangs in the balance now whether this child she is carrying is the legitimate boy Henry seeks or just another girl," she explained in a hushed tone, though they were safely in the comfort of her own residence, "With Katherine no longer around, the king may not feel it as necessary to keep Queen Anne if she continues to fail him."

"You mean," Henry summarised slowly, "That Father may choose to divorce her? As he did Katherine, if this child is not his heir?"

Bessie shrugged, "It is only what I have heard whispered in the breeze. I know many seek her downfall, men who are in the king's ear. I am quite sure this is the queen's final chance to come through, or risk losing everything she has obtained."

Henry looked up then as a figure emerged from the side gate and headed towards them.

Bessie followed his gaze and smiled to see her new husband approaching, a flush coming to her cheeks.

Her son noticed her endearing reaction, "Do you sometimes wonder what might have happened had Father chosen you instead of Queen Anne?"

Bessie continued observing Edward as he strode over casually, his hands in his pockets, "For your sake, perhaps," she admitted, tearing her eyes off her husband and looking up at her grown son, "If only to grant you what your heart so greatly desires."

Henry met her gaze, but he did not like to see the pity in her eyes.

"But for myself," she continued, as Edward Fiennes de Clinton met them and took Bessie's hand in his and brought it to his lips, "I have everything that I would ever want."

Henry watched the wholesome exchange, touched by his mother's ability to be happy with the life she had gained, despite the fact she could have had so much more.

"I am happy for you, Lady Mother," Henry said in earnest.

And he realised in that moment – as touching as it was – that without the only girl he loved as his wife, he would not be satisfied with a simple life; and that, unless he achieved his goal, his ambition would never be sated.

24th January 1536
Greenwich Palace, London

In preparation for the May Day tournaments that occurred each year, King Henry had taken time out of his busy schedule to train for the jousting event he would partake in.

He made his way to the tiltyard at Greenwich Palace with his friend and advisor Charles Brandon, the two men discussing that Spring's entertainments. At forty-four, King Henry still felt very much able and willing to partake in most every athletic event, physical activities always having been not only his forte but also his preferred means of entertainment. He felt most alive when adrenaline rushed through his body. Or, Charles knew, when he had a new lady in his life.

As he was being dressed in his armour under the canopy by the tiltyard, he and Charles spoke of unimportant matters, Charles noticing that his king was laughing easily and steering clear of political discourse. He wondered, as Henry walked past him and towards his horse – a courser – to commence the practice joust, if his mood was indeed light-hearted due to his newfound interest in one of Queen Anne's ladies, or if he was distracting himself from the fact that it was his first wife's funeral in but five days' time.

Charles sincerely hoped it was the former, for though Katherine of Aragon's passing had left many in mourning, Henry could not afford to be distracted.

Charles observed from the shade of one of the tents as the two jousters rode the rings to develop their accuracy and coordination skills. After some time, they took their places to commence their practice passes.

Charles looked around himself briefly then, to find a seat to perch on, the sound of galloping horse hooves behind him, when he suddenly heard a bloodcurdling cry and a horrific *crunching* sound. He whirled around to a terrifying sight: the king flat on his back on the dusty ground, his courser trotting frantically to-and-fro, dust clouding Charles' vision.

His blood ran cold, and the hysteria that followed was staggering.

The king!
Fetch the physicians!
Hurry, hurry! Take the horse away!
Be careful, don't crowd him.

Charles Brandon rushed over and pushed past the few who had gathered, then gently removed the king's helmet. Henry's eyes were closed, and his breathing was shallow.

"Bring a gurney!" he called into the crowd of ambassadors and guards in attendance at the training, "And hurry up that physician!"

Later, once the king had been transferred from the ground to his private chambers, the physicians examined him in hushed voices, the old men hovering nearby, hesitant to move him too much for fear of injuring him further.

And news of the king's fall began to bleed through the walls of the castle, whispers of his imminent death churning through the air like a poisonous smog.

"He fell?" Queen Anne said in horror, as reports of her husband's accident reached her, "Where is he? Is he hurt?!"

The Imperial ambassador raised his hand, "He is with the physicians, Your Highness. But he has not spoken in nearly two hours."

Anne's frightened eyes met the ambassador's, then her stepson Henry Fitzroy's, "Is he awake?"

Henry looked to the ambassador, who did not answer, for he did not wish to worry her further.

The queen fretted before them nevertheless, her face crumbling with concern, her ladies, including the king's rumoured mistress Jane Seymour, *shushing* her like a child and mumbling soothingly.

Henry watched as she brought one hand to her temple, her eyes scrunched together as though she might wake herself from this terrible nightmare. Then she pressed her other hand to her rounded belly, and Henry thought of how she ought to contain herself, lest she risk causing harm to the child.

It was in that moment, in that swift train of thought, that Henry realised what good fortune had befallen him with this tragedy. And before he could stop himself or talk himself out of doing something he knew he would later regret, he stepped forward.

"He is likely to die," he told the queen monotonously, unable to recognise his own voice, unable to believe he had just said that. And he was suddenly reminded of how he and George Blount had goaded one another, how each jibe had felt like a dart of poison by the end of their friendship.

He sensed the Imperial ambassador frowning next to him, saw some of her ladies look up in horror. And yet he could not stop, though his mind was telling him that this was a terrible idea.

"What will you do then?" he continued, his eyes wide in disbelief at himself, his tone cutting, "If he does not wake?"

"If the king dies?" Anne Boleyn replied, her wet eyes shining with fear and something else Henry could not identify.

She returned to sobbing then, loud, ominous wails soaked in panic, and Henry took a step back before heading out the door with the ambassador, who shot him a perplexed look.

Henry cast one final glance over his shoulder before exiting the room, not only to avoid the ambassador's confused stare, but also to fully take in the scene he had helped to create, for the guilt of his actions was already eating him up inside, and he wished with all his heart that he hadn't stooped so low.

29th January 1536

In the days after the king's fall, a ripple effect of tragedies ensued which would seal the fate of many.

"The queen has miscarried," Hal informed Henry, once again taking his chances on his friend's future over that of his cousin's. And Henry wondered, as his stomach churned at the news, if Hal would think twice about siding with him if he knew the part Henry had played in causing the queen's agitation.

"Miscarried?" Henry echoed, stunned, feeling lightheaded as the guilt overwhelmed him.

"They are saying it was caused by her worry for the king."

"But the king is fine," Henry insisted, though it wasn't completely true.

The fall had not been life-threatening in the end, Henry's father waking shortly after Queen Anne had been informed of the accident. But it had been bad enough to have burst an old ulcer on the king's leg, which – after five days of care – had not managed to close up or show any signs of healing.

Hal shrugged, unable to understand what had caused the queen's distress, "Whatever the reason, she has miscarried once again. And if rumours are to be believed, it was another boy."

Henry exhaled ruefully at that, pressing his thumb and forefinger into the corners of his scrunched-up eyes. Then nausea crept in, and he leaned forward, his hands on his knees, to keep from being sick.

Hal, surprised by his reaction, pressed a hand on his back.

"Hey," he said, "Are you ill?"

Henry straightened himself and inhaled deeply, his eyes remaining closed.

"No," he assured Hal, "I am well."

Then, desperate to shake some of the overwhelming shame that he felt, Henry's mind searched for anything he could deflect blame onto, "I cannot help but think the Seymour girl to somehow be responsible," he muttered, gulping down air.

"Responsible?" Hal frowned, "How so?"

"Not directly," Henry explained, desperate to make the idea stick, "But the king's interest in her is plain to see. The whole court knows he is courting her. Much the same way he once courted Queen Anne."

Hal cocked his head to one side, irked to hear it though he knew it to be true.

"Perhaps it is fear of being replaced that caused the miscarriage," Hal concluded slowly, as Henry had hoped, "And not fear for the king's life at all."

"Perhaps," Henry replied, eager to absolve himself of any fault, though he was certain this shame would never leave him.

March 1536

Following Queen Anne's tragic loss, it was suddenly crystal clear that the king no longer wished to continue within his marriage to her, and he made that widely known by distancing himself from her whenever possible. Just as he had done with Katherine of Aragon.

He refused to acknowledge her presence at banquets, though they sat side by side. He spent all his time either with his council members or with his closest confidants, never again opting for a private moment with the woman who he had done so much for to attain.

Henry felt sick to think of his involvement, however small or true it may have been.

What a dangerous thing jealousy was. For it was that alone which had led him to taunt the woman, his zeal urging him to take what he believed to be his.

You would do well to establish yourself.

Hal's words from years ago suddenly sprung to mind, as though to alleviate his conscience. He shook his mind clear. What he had done had been underhanded and wrong. And no amount of reasoning would make him feel any better.

2nd May 1536

Queen Anne and her ladies were enjoying the fine Spring air and feeling greatly entertained at a tennis match when a messenger arrived summoning her to present herself to the King's Privy Council.

"The king has asked for me?" Queen Anne inquired, her stomach dropping as she wondered if this was good or bad news.

"No, Your Grace," the messenger replied, shaking his head, "He orders for you to go to the council chambers. To present yourself to the Privy Council."

Bad news, she surmised.

Anne cleared her throat before rising from her seat, "Tell the king's council that the queen is underway," and she watched as the messenger sped off ahead.

After a moment to compose herself, Anne made her way up the path and into the palace, her throat tightening with each step, for she knew that the king was much displeased with her, and that his interest in the Seymour woman had grown intense in the wake of Anne's most recent loss.

Every fibre of her body screamed for her to run, and yet she entered the council chamber with her head held high, remembering how Katherine of Aragon herself had stood her ground with much poise and elegance in the legatine court so many years ago. Anne would look to her this day, the woman she had replaced, for she was very much aware of how their fates had grown so similar.

Whatever the King's Council might throw at her today, Anne would deny it. A pre-contract, a dispute over her virginity, some minor offence. She would admit to none of it, of course, for she would protect her daughter's birthright no matter the cost.

Just as Katherine of Aragon had done.

The thought pierced her heart, finally understanding why her predecessor had fought so hard for her title. It had never been about the riches, the power, the status. But for her child.

Anne braced herself, then relaxed slightly at the sight of her own uncle the Duke of Norfolk, for surely, he would speak for her no matter what accusations may come her way.

But then the three members of the privy council spoke, spouting words which made no sense to Anne Boleyn.

Treason. Adultery. Incest.

And she realised that her husband would not be as lenient with her as he had been with Katherine of Aragon. He wanted her gone to make way for a new queen. And this time, Henry VIII would not wait seven years before ridding himself of his second wife.

And just like the one who came before her, Anne Boleyn, too, would never get to say goodbye to her daughter.

The arrest of the Queen of England came as a shock to everyone, including Henry Fitzroy.

Even after he had heard of the musician Mark Smeaton's arrest and torture, he could not believe that his father would go so far as to arrest and try the woman he had once professed to love above any other.

He wanted her gone, that much was clear. The whole court now knew that the king and his queen were no longer inseparable, as they had once been. It was a striking déjà vu for those who had witnessed the king's love for his first wife dwindle at the end of their twenty-four-year marriage. But this outcome was quite different. And nobody could have predicted it.

The way Queen Anne had been accosted by the king's councillors, accused of treason, adultery and incest, then thrown into the Tower of London...that was not love, Henry thought.

He remembered how his mother and Gil used to look at each other. How his mother now looked at her new husband. Surely, they would never wish to hurt one another. Even Henry, who did not love his own wife Mary Howard, could never imagine wanting to harm her in order to replace her. Or for any reason at that.

But then, Henry thought, if his father *was* going down this route, perhaps the accusations were true after all? For as Supreme Head of the Church of England, his father could very easily annul his marriage to Anne Boleyn with but a wave of his hand. So then, if she was innocent, why wouldn't he?

Henry continued uneasy throughout the rest of the day, surprised at how much his heart went out to the woman, torn between his newfound empathy for her, and believing what the king was presenting as facts against her.

The rest of the court was just as uneasy, speaking in hushed whispers and looking around with uncertainty in their eyes, wondering who would be called to be interrogated next. Wondering if they would be racked for information, as Mark Smeaton had been.

Later that day, Henry was summoned to his father's chambers, where he found his flustered king pacing up and down the length of his room.

As soon as his son entered, King Henry pulled him into a hard embrace, knocking air out of the young man's lungs at the suddenness of it.

"Oh!" young Henry exclaimed, startled by the unusual display of affection.

He could not remember the last time his father had held him like this, except for his one early memory of the king raising him high in the air as a baby before crushing him against his chest, his bejewelled jacket digging into Henry's plump cheek as he'd giggled.

This embrace felt strange however, for as an adult he had no longer expected to be held as such by his father. And it put Henry on high alert.

The king let go of him then and held him at arm's length, searching his face for a moment.

"What is it, Father?" Henry asked before the king could speak.

His father's chin wobbled theatrically, causing Henry to frown, perplexed.

"You ought to thank God," the king confessed then, his face twisted in anger, "for having escaped from the hands of that woman!"

Henry's eyes widened, "Escaped?" he asked, "Lord Father, what do you mean? What has happened?"

King Henry turned from his son, ran a hand through his thinning hair, "She was planning your death by poison!" he explained, "Yours *and* the Lady Mary's!"

At that, Henry stiffened, "Poison?" he parroted, suddenly fearful. Suddenly feeling a little less guilty for his part in her downfall.

The king, having heard the boy's fearful tone, approached him once more, "Do not fret. She is in the Tower. She cannot hurt you now."

The accusation hung heavily in the air, and Henry couldn't help but think back on the other times Anne Boleyn had tried to remove him from her path to greatness, from her children's path to supersede him. The crazed stallion was one thing, arranging his marriage to her cousin another.

But would she really have stooped so low as to try to *poison* him? And his half-sister?

Henry was not sure he could believe it. Almost didn't want to imagine it.

But then...whyever would his father lie?

15th May 1536

A case of incest and adultery was quickly assembled against Anne Boleyn.

King Henry's new favourite, Thomas Cromwell, had been given the task to gather as much damning information against her, and given her informal and playful interactions with many of the court, it did not look promising for an innocent verdict.

The king was not present at the trials, sending Henry Fitzroy in his stead to take his place and to oversee the proceedings. He, as well as several others including Henry Percy, Anne Boleyn's former beloved, sat as members of the jury at her trial. And though she and Fitzroy had not seen eye to eye throughout the years, the king's son was surprised to feel sorry for the poor woman as she stood before so many great lords and proclaimed her innocence. She had not been allowed to produce any witnesses in her defence, or to summon a lawyer to fight her case. And, to the young man at least, that in itself spoke volumes as to the truth.

"To have her burned would make it an even greater spectacle," Charles Brandon told his friend King Henry, adding his two cents into the discussion at hand, "Executing a Queen of England has never been done before. You must be seen to show her some dignity at least."

Henry VIII inhaled deeply and closed his eyes as he stood unseeingly before the window of his private chambers. He knew his friend was right, and yet the hatred he felt for the woman was so raw he cared little for what the people would think.

"To be burned at the stake is common practice for female traitors to the crown," the king added defiantly.

Charles exhaled in frustration, "It would not be seen as very goodly."

"I don't give a damn how it may look!" the king bellowed then, turning to face Charles.

But the older man only cocked his head to one side, looking back at his friend as though to challenge his statement. For they both knew the king cared very much about appearances, in fact.

Henry simmered down when he spied Charles' look. He sighed.

"Yes, of course you are right, Charles," he said, walking towards him, "But there were *many* witnesses that day when she spoke of my demise. She said, and I quote: 'if something were to happen to the king'…if that is not imagining – nay, *plotting* – my death, then I don't know what is! To speak of my passing is treason!"

The Treasons Act of 1534 that King Henry had passed, the Act many had feared would lead to innocent deaths, seemed to be doing just that. For even Charles, who had never accepted Anne Boleyn as queen, could believe that what she had said had not been in spite. Regardless of what Charles thought of the woman, she was not a fool.

And yet, Charles did not believe her capable of salvation, King Henry being too angered by her failures to produce a son, as well as for her refusing to rein in her headstrong personality. The very same personality that the king had once found so alluring.

And so, Charles kept his mouth shut, allowing his friend to come to his own conclusion. For at this point the matter was no longer about *if* she would die, but rather *how*.

Chapter 18

19th May 1536
Tower of London

  Just four years after meeting with King Francis I at Calais to see Anne Boleyn publicly accepted as Queen of England, King Henry VIII asked his son to attend her execution at the Tower of London.

Henry Fitzroy stood among the sizeable crowd that had gathered to watch Queen Anne Boleyn's end. He had been ordered to attend her execution in lieu of his father, representing him just as he had done for those monks not long ago.

His presence revealed much to those who spotted him beside the Duke of Norfolk and the Duke of Suffolk, for the king's son's attendance at such an event meant that the monarch was in complete agreement with what was about to happen.

Though her execution had been deemed as private in contrast to those that had occurred some days ago – Mark Smeaton and the queen's own brother George Boleyn having been found guilty of knowing the queen carnally and been beheaded for their sins – Henry judged there were still roughly a thousand people waiting for her at the scaffold.

A low mumble and some gasps sounded at precisely eight o'clock in the morning, and Henry turned his head just as Anne Boleyn emerged, flanked by four of her ladies.

He watched as she was escorted through the courtyard of the Tower to the new scaffold in what Henry could only describe as a grim procession. And to his surprise, she appeared to head to her execution with an untroubled countenance.

His stomach clenched as she caught his eye briefly, and the memory of how he had provoked her not long ago flashed in his mind. He looked away, shame burning his cheeks for his part in this, though he could never have known his single remark would have had such an effect.

Then he remembered what his father had told him she had been plotting. To poison him and his half-sister, the king's only other children, in order to clear the way for her own daughter to claim the first place in the line of succession. And he raised his head to return her hard gaze.

Did he believe it? Henry wasn't sure.

There was a small part of him that thought her capable of considering such an act. There were enough rumours flying around of late that she had even poisoned the late Queen Katherine…

But Henry inhaled and pushed the thoughts aside. It no longer mattered, for whether she was guilty or innocent, her fate was sealed.

The king's son noticed Anne's piercing eyes flick to the man standing ramrod-straight beside Henry then, and he followed her gaze to his father-in-law, the queen's own uncle. The Duke of Norfolk stared back stony-faced, uncaring – or perhaps extremely good at hiding his true emotions – that his niece was to die right before his eyes.

Henry swallowed and tore his gaze from his father-in-law. He would never forget the trials, where Norfolk had agreed with his peers and condemned his niece and nephew to die.

Many other earls, lords, and ladies of the realm attended this most extraordinary event. Even the Mayor of London stood among the crowd. And when she climbed the steps – which were draped in black cloth and covered in straw – and appeared upon the scaffold, a great murmur rose from the masses.

"The queen has never looked so beautiful," a Portuguese ambassador in front of Henry whispered to himself.

There was no block, Henry had noticed earlier, for Anne was not to be beheaded like her brother before her.

The axe can be messy, Henry remembered his father warning him before attending Thomas More's execution. But to the boy's relief, More's beheading had been proficient.

The king, following Charles Brandon's sound advice, had opted against burning the queen at the stake, and in his pity for her decided to grant her a swifter ending. His benevolence had been noted by the public, just as the king had hoped, and a French swordsman had been requested, to commit the act in a more elegant fashion than a common beheading by the axe.
Instead of laying her head on a block, the queen was to kneel upright for the blow. But before she did so, she opened her mouth to speak.

"Good Christian people," she said, her voice clear and concise despite knowing they would be her last, "I have come not to preach a sermon. I have come here to die. For according to the law I am judged to die, and therefore I will speak nothing against it! I have come hither to accuse no man, nor to speak of that whereof I am accused and condemned to die –"
A woman blubbered before Henry, and he frowned at her, willing her to cry quietly so that he may hear the queen's final words.

" – I pray God save the king and send him long to reign over you, for there was never a gentler nor more merciful prince."
To Henry's horror, a chuckle escaped one of the members of the vast crowd, and he briefly searched their faces to see if he could spot the wrongdoer.
With a frown, he returned his attention to the matter ahead.

" – And thus I take my leave of this world, and I heartily desire you all to pray for me!"
And with that, she knelt before the crowd and mumbled a prayer as she was blindfolded. Henry was certain he heard a tiny squeal of panic escape her at the feel of the blindfold being tied behind her head, and the world turning dark.
Her hands were clasped before her, and Henry noticed that they were shaking. Her brave stance was breaking, and underneath the blindfold, her face showed her fear.
The crowd watched as the French executioner raised his sword, some crying silently, some grinning with delight, many staring wide-eyed in pure fascination.

And then the sword came down, and took her head clean off.

June 1536

Just one day after Queen Anne's execution, King Henry had ridden to his new love and asked for her hand in marriage.
Henry Fitzroy had briefly considered, at the time, just how heartless one had to be to do such a thing but a day after beheading the woman that had come before. Then he deliberated how terrified Jane Seymour must have been to receive the king and to act as though everything was right in the world. All the while knowing that he had murdered his former wife in order to have her.

"How does it feel to be back at court? Under a Catholic queen, no less?" Henry now asked his mother, Bessie Blount, who had been selected to attend the new queen as one of her ladies, just as she had served Queen Katherine two decades earlier.

"Surprisingly, much the same as it did during Queen Katherine's reign," Bessie admitted, "The return of the gable hood suits me just fine," and she touched the beautiful maroon hood upon her head.

It had been just two weeks since the king's third wedding had taken place on the 30th of May, and with the former queen dead and buried, it appeared almost as if the king were trying to erase her from history all together. He had removed all signs of Anne Boleyn that Henry could tell. Her royal emblem of the falcon that Henry VIII had once so admired had been removed from the palaces and castles just days after her death. Any portraits of her had been burned in a great bonfire, along with most of her other possessions.

Even the former queen's preferred fashion statement – the French hood – had been requested not to be worn, since the new queen preferred the more traditional style of the gable hood. Queen Jane had, no doubt, returned to the English style hood partly as some strategic tactic to separate herself as much as possible from her predecessor; the French hood having been deemed by many as scandalous and wanton. And Henry could only imagine that Queen Jane wished to maintain her innocence and virtue in the eyes of the king in any way she could.

"I see your wife has returned as lady-in-waiting to Queen Jane," Bessie added, casting a glance at the girl in question, "I am glad the king has not extended his rage to the Howard family. But perhaps that is somewhat to do with you being married into it."

Henry shrugged, no longer certain of how his father's mind worked, or why he did what he did.

"Do you think he will succeed now?" Henry asked his mother quietly then, turning his back on the few courtiers surrounding them, so that only Bessie would hear.

She knew what he meant, of course. For it had also been on her mind.

Bessie looked over her son's shoulder – which was not an easy task, since he towered over her now at over six feet tall – and examined the new queen. As though she may predict her fertility with the naked eye.

"She may be capable, yes," she admitted casually, "Though she is no longer a young woman."

Henry nodded, turning to stand beside his mother once again and following her gaze to the smiling queen across the room, surrounded by several nobles and ladies.

"It could be months before she conceives," Bessie reassured her son, "And even then, who's to say it will be a boy?"

Henry's eyebrow twitched, "I cannot simply sit about and wait any longer. Father must make certain a plan for me."

Bessie smiled thinly, "There is not much you can do but wait, my son."

But, Henry thought, that was not entirely true. He had come this far. He would not give up yet.

And he allowed his gaze to drift back to the new queen and her entourage, his eyes settling pensively on the girl who would call herself his wife.

25th June 1536

Parliament was recalled, and Anne Boleyn's daughter Elizabeth was excluded from the line of succession. Much like the king's eldest daughter, Mary, had been.

The Lady Mary, who had previously been shunned from court and reduced to no more than a maid to her half-sister Elizabeth at Hatfield House, finally signed the oath to the Act of Supremacy, two years after its passing.

Truthfully, Henry thought, it was a miracle the lady had not been put to death already for her disobedience, like so many others had for doing far less.

But Henry Fitzroy knew just how desperate their father was for successors. Desperate enough to have elevated him – a mere bastard – to the peerage. Desperate enough to break from Catholic Rome in order to pursue a fresh marriage.

King Henry VIII couldn't risk wasting any of his children. Not when he'd already buried so many and was yet to have any more since Elizabeth's birth in 1533.

And who knew? Perhaps this new wife of his would be as incapable of birthing a son as the previous two.

With the signing of the oath – as well as Jane Seymour's advocating for her – the Lady Mary was returned to the court and reunited with her father.

Henry wasn't sure when father and daughter had last seen each other, but their reunion was as forced as could be. He'd watched with heavy-lidded eyes as the king had kissed his daughter's hand and she'd curtsied to him. Henry had taken some quiet contentment in noticing a slight twitch of Mary's upper lip as the stench of their father's ulcerous leg had hit her nostrils, and how she'd almost failed to disguise her disgust.

Henry couldn't help it, but he felt threatened by his half-sister's return to the public eye.

Mary was beloved by many, and now that the new queen had taken her under her wing, he wondered if she would become a problem.

He covered his mouth with his fist as a dry cough escaped him then, the tickle in his throat continuing to irk him since that morning.

Henry would have to observe Queen Jane and the Lady Mary closely if he wished not to be side-lined by some sudden change of heart of their father's. After all, Henry knew all too well how King Henry's love and affection could change to suspicion and hatred in a heartbeat.

26th June 1536

"Lady Mary," Henry said in greeting, bowing his head at his older half-sister.

"Brother," she replied with a half-smile.

She did not dip into a curtsy, though technically, he was now of slightly higher rank than she. Since all three of the king's children had been deemed illegitimate, and he was the only male.

Henry noted it with a crooked smile.

"I am glad to see you returned to court," he said, though he wasn't sure she would believe it.

Mary breathed a small laugh. It seemed she did not.

Henry looked over her shoulder at her two ladies – Cecily and Frances they were called, if he remembered correctly – then back at his sister's hard face.

"Would you walk with me a while?"

Mary considered it for a beat, then nodded and took the arm he had presented.

She glanced over her shoulder to inform her ladies she wished for them to stay at a distance, sensing her brother's wish for a private moment.

They walked along the hallway in silence until sunlight washed over them in the open-air courtyard. Henry led his sister along the path, then cleared his throat once a group of young noblemen had walked past.

"I have a proposition I wanted to run by you," he said, "One that I believe may be beneficial to us both obtaining what we want."

"And what is that?" Mary asked.

Henry cast her a glance, and Mary smiled knowingly.

He observed her then as she stared ahead.

Mary Tudor was no great beauty, not by any stretch of the imagination. Her lips were thin and her eyes, though blue, were surrounded by almost invisible eyelashes and thin, auburn brows. Her cheeks were rosy but gaunt, and her skin was that of a woman much older than her twenty years. Granted, she had been through a lot of heartache In the past few years, but even without all that, Henry could remember she had always been plain, even in childhood.

That being said, her elegance and strength shone through. One could tell by the way she held herself, with her shoulders back and her chin raised, that she believed herself to be of royal and pure birth, no matter what their father said. And it was that conviction within her that had attracted Henry to his newest idea.

"You and I both want the crown," he stated matter-of-factly.

Mary only nodded, then smiled at Lady Rochford as she and another lady walked past.

Henry continued quietly, "And you and I are both now of equal level."

He felt her arm tense in his, but she did not disagree out loud.

"What is your point, brother?" she said instead.

Henry chuckled, "It's funny you continue to call me that. Because my proposition is one where you may have to revisit that."

Mary frowned and stopped, turned to look at him. Her ladies stopped a few paces behind, still out of earshot.

"What is this?" she asked, a crease appearing between her brows.

Henry licked his dry lips. It was a tricky plan. But one he believed in. And one he hoped would take shape.

"My marriage to Mary Howard is unfulfilled," he said, "She and I, we do not want the same thing. I respect her greatly, but her connection to Queen Anne is a stain on my reputation."

At the mention of Anne Boleyn, Henry noticed Mary's face souring.

He continued, "I could request an annulment. I believe our Lord Father would grant me it."

A moment of heavy silence pulsated between them as the words hung in the air.

"We could reawaken Father's old plan for us," Henry went on, forcing himself to take her hand, "We need not be at odds with one another. Father is yet without a son. What are the chances that the new queen will give him one? And if she does, the odds of the child surviving to adulthood are slim. We should unite, his daughter and his son. Together we can achieve what we both want *and* save the Tudor dynasty."

His cheeks were flushed by the end of his speech, his breathing a little uneven. He hadn't realised until he'd said it just how much hope he truly had for this plan.

Mary was looking up at him. Though she was older by three years, Henry had inherited their father's stature. And at seventeen years old, he had stretched into his full height of six feet two inches, just like their father. In fact, if Mary squinted her eyes, her brother could pass for their father in his youth, a fact which made his proposal all the more disconcerting.

She gently removed her hand from his, "I shall think on it, brother."

They both flinched at the use of her label for him, for though they indeed shared a father, Henry's suggestion had turned them into something else. And if Mary decided to agree with the pursuit of this incestuous proposal, they would have to come to terms with the idea of becoming each other's betrothed.

*

The Lady Mary had not even dared to share her brother's repulsive idea with her ladies-in-waiting, though they had always known all her secrets. But this one felt different.
This secret felt not only dirty, but also treasonous.
And she decided to use it to her advantage in regaining her father's favour.

"Lord Father," the king's eldest daughter said as she curtsied deeply and smiled at the man whom she loved and hated in equal measures.

"My darling daughter!" the man called as he hobbled towards her, and she stifled her breathing to avoid inhaling that awful stench that surrounded her father of late.

"What brings you here?" King Henry asked as he fell into his seat by the open window. His groom knelt before him, and once the king had resumed his seat, the boy began massaging his ulcerous leg.

Mary stepped towards them but remained standing, her hands clasped elegantly before her, her rosary beads hanging from between them, as if to remind her father of her staunch beliefs. He glanced at them, the cross dangling gently, and smiled lazily up at her. And she thought she saw a challenge in his eyes.

But she wasn't here for that. Never would Mary dare to contest what he had done to her mother, for she knew it would lead to nothing. And she needed him on her side now as she built herself back up.

"I come with news of your son," she said, looking down at the aging king.

Henry blinked, "What of him?" he asked, and Mary tried to pretend not to have heard the pride in his voice.

She raised her chin, "He came to me with a proposition I have to share with you," she said, "One that I believe you will find hard to hear."

The king heard his daughter's warning, and he turned to the groom and waved his hand, dismissing him.

They watched as the servant left the king's chambers and the guard by the door followed, closing the door behind them both. Once alone, Mary sat down facing the king.

Henry VIII frowned deeply at his eldest child, the girl who could have amounted to so much had he given her a chance.

"Speak," he said, feeling his distrust twitching to life like the spark from striking flint.

"Your son," she said tentatively, "He has come to me with the most incredible idea. I was rather taken aback, given that he is already married and I his sister and you with a new wife. It was rather a strange concept, and one which left me uncomfortable, for the way that he proposed it – it suggested to me that he had been concocting this plan without Your Majesty's consent?"

Henry shook his head, the nightcap on his head making him look old and feeble, "Well, tell me girl, as you can see I do not know of what you speak!"

His paranoia was flaring up, much like the infection in his leg. Mary smiled, she knew she had him then. Eating out of the palm of her hand. And she savoured the moment for as long as she dared, enjoying seeing *him* feeling lost and vulnerable for once.

"Forgive me, Father," she mumbled, "I thought you must know, for surely why else would he have hatched such an elaborate scheme if not with your knowledge?"

The king's eyes narrowed.

"He asked for my hand in marriage," Mary finally explained, "With the understanding that you would allow for an annulment from his wife Mary Howard. Tell me, Father, is there any substance to this? Do you wish to pursue this path once more? For whatever you shall rule, I will obey, as I always have. But if you have no knowledge of this, then perhaps your son is getting a little ahead of himself."

The king tore his gaze from his eldest child and stared blankly at the floor between them, his pale blue eyes wide as she tried to understand everything he had just heard.

"Henry wishes for an annulment. And to marry you? His sister?" he muttered, as if disturbed by the concept. Though he and Mary both knew that it had been his own suggestion of it years ago that had caused his son to revisit the idea.

But Mary remained quiet, allowing her father to reach his own conclusion. She could already see his mind working away as his eyes flicked to-and-fro, his grey eyebrows twitching in thought.

His son, Henry VIII deliberated, going behind his king's back, making plans to assert himself?

He didn't know what to make of it. But it aroused that old suspicion in him once again.

Perhaps Anne had been right about him…

Henry didn't know whether to be proud, or worried.

But in the end, he settled for the latter.

Chapter 19

Paranoia.

It was something which no king could avoid during his reign. Even the most established and admired rulers had occasions in which they would question the loyalty of those surrounding them. Whether it be age, or illness, or mental instability, a weak claim, or a weak succession, something would always cause a monarch to worry.

And in Henry VIII's case, all of those applied.

But what was he to do with this news? This news that his son was plotting – against him? – behind his back? – without consulting him?

He wondered briefly if this was how his father had felt in the final years of his life? When a young Henry VIII had made the entire court and country swoon with his good looks and charm and promise of a better future?

But Henry Fitzroy was no Henry VIII. He wasn't *as* accepted by the people, nor was he as well liked.

Or was he?

King Henry wasn't sure anymore. For all that he had put his country through in pursuit of that *whore* Anne Boleyn had caused a rift between the public and their sovereign.

Perhaps they really *would* support an uprising, to replace their dilapidated king with his own bastard son.

Henry knocked back the cup of wine he had been staring into as he'd pondered. Then refilled it.

But what if he agreed to his son's proposition of marrying his half-sister Mary, and thereby naming them as his joint heirs? Would that be enough for Fitzroy? Would it quash any potential ideas he might have of usurpation?

Henry nodded to himself, he believed it would, for it was all his son had ever wanted – to be accepted as worthy.

The king rubbed his hand over his tired face. He had thought Mary and Henry's union a wonderful idea years ago, had even gotten the pope's approval for it...

If only he'd accepted it and given up his chase of that woman. He shook his head, Anne Boleyn had cost him a lot. And he'd gotten nothing in return for it.

Well, he told himself as he took another large gulp of his wine, not nothing. The riches and power he'd obtained from the dissolution of the churches was not something to be sniffed at. But could he really go down this route again? To marry his son to his daughter and leave the country to them? To rule as a brother-sister king and queen?

Or would he throw this opportunity away once again and put all his faith into his new wife, the gentle and loving Jane Seymour who, after already two months of marriage had not yet shown any signs of conception...

King Henry VIII was at a crossroads. And he knew not which road he should take.

Only that one would lead him to his goal. While the other would lead him to a difficult decision, one where the king might have to eliminate he who would threaten his reign.

July 1536

It was finally happening. The very thing Henry Fitzroy had been praying for his entire life.

He should have been there, when the new Act of Succession was put before Parliament. But he had been too ill to attend due to a dull pain in his chest and a wretched cough that had come out of nowhere one morning.

This new Act had been exactly what he had waited for his whole life, the one that would enable the king to nominate any one of his children as his heir no matter their legitimacy.

Everyone knew what that meant: that it would be he – the king's bastard son – that would be named as the heir to the throne.

But by some twisted turn of events, Henry – who had been in good health all of his life – had not been able to see it be passed with his own eyes.

He had lain abed now for two weeks, ever since he last visited his father for a private supper. The king and his court had left London on their summer progress the following day, to escape the city during the more dangerous months of heat and potential plague. But young Henry had been too weak to travel, and his cough continued to ravage him from the inside out.

He was told by his mother when she visited a few days later, her cheeks tear-stained and her hand on his arm as she sat by his bed, that Parliament had passed the Act. He'd seen her beautiful face blurring in and out as he'd listened, fighting for consciousness.

But Henry had managed to smile weakly at the news, before a wet cough had consumed him and he'd spluttered into a handkerchief before inhaling a shuddered breath.

His sister Elizabeth came to see him one afternoon, he thought, although he couldn't be sure, for he had dreamt a lot in the last few days, and he could no longer distinguish between what was real and what wasn't. His fever and headache had made him delirious.

"You got your wish," he thought she had whispered as she'd sniffled, "all you have ever prayed for has come to pass."

She was right, Henry thought as he exhaled happily and closed his eyes. Their father had seen his son's worth.

Finally…right at the end.

And just in time for Henry Fitzroy, the king's bastard son, to die a happy man.

Epilogue:

Just as Henry Fitzroy had predicted, removing her from the warmer weather of France would be the end of the girl he had loved.

Princess Madeleine of Valois, who had been frail since birth and raised in the mild climate to protect her from the cold, had caught the eye of King James V of Scots the same year that she had received news that the first boy she had loved had died of what was believed to have been consumption.

She had tucked the memory of Henry away upon hearing the dreadful news, for though she had sometimes wondered what might have been had he remained in France, she was now a grown woman of sixteen and ready for marriage.

King James had originally come to France to meet another lady, Marie of Bourbon, but upon his arrival he had been enamoured and smitten by Madeleine's delicate beauty, promptly asking King Francis I for her hand in marriage instead.

Madeleine had been flattered by the attention from the handsome king, who with his red hair and charismatic grin had reminded her of Prince Henry.

They had married on the 1st of January 1537 at Notre Dame Cathedral in Paris and celebrated their union for four months before setting sail to Scotland in the spring. It had been the happiest time of Madeleine's life.

But Madeleine had not long survived the harsh climates of her husband's country, and though she had arrived to what would be her new homeland in good spirits, kissing the very ground upon her arrival, the Princess of Valois had died in her new husband's arms just six months after their swift marriage.

The very same illness that was believed to have killed her first love, sending her to an early grave almost exactly a year later.

End of Book 5

Author's note:

As always, I'd like to remind the reader that this is a work of fiction, and while it is based on the life of Henry Fitzroy, some aspects of the story have been altered or fictionalised.
Some of the creative liberties I took include:
- Henry Fitzroy's strained relationship with his uncle George Blount. There is no evidence to suggest that they didn't always get on.
- His romance with Madeleine of Valois is sadly also fictitious, although he did spend almost a year at the French court, where they did refer to him as 'Prince Henry'. Princess Madeleine being in poor health, however, is accurate, as is her initially broken-off betrothal to King James V of Scotland, and their eventual marriage. Which was subsequently what led to her untimely death just six months later, due to tuberculosis.
- Henry Fitzroy's father King Henry VIII also did not fear usurpation at the hands of his illegitimate son. That plotline was entirely fictional.
- Henry Fitzroy's involvement in Anne Boleyn's panic following King Henry's accident in 1536 is also fictitious, for he was not even present when she was informed. Though it is thought that her worry for the king's wellbeing was what led to her having her final miscarriage, but Henry Fitzroy is innocent of any taunting of her.

However, a lot of the story is historically accurate, as I believe it is important to stay true to history as much as possible. Any alterations I did make never steered the true history off course. Some things I stayed true to include – but are not limited to:
- The theory that Bessie Blount's daughter, Elizabeth, was King Henry VIII's child. Historian and author Elizabeth Norton suggested the likelihood that Bessie Blount's daughter was Henry VIII's, and not Gilbert Tailboys', due to the fact that, while Elizabeth was born in 1520 (therefore likely conceived in 1519), the first piece of evidence we have of

Bessie's marriage to Gilbert is not until two years later in June 1522 where 'Bessie was recorded as Gilbert's wife for the first time'. With this knowledge Norton argues that the king continued his affair with Bessie after Henry Fitzroy's birth and fathered another child by her, this time a girl, who he had no interest in claiming.
- It is also true that Henry Fitzroy is said to have had a lisp in his youth and that his first tutor, Palsgrave, had believed it would become less noticeable 'when his adult teeth come in'.
- The occasion when Anne Boleyn gifted a young Henry Fitzroy a horse, which was 'very ill to ride, and of worse condition' is also true, and according to historian Mathew Lyons, Fitzroy had to 'immediately regift it'. Lyons describes Anne Boleyn and Henry Fitzroy's relationship as 'testy', which is further supported by her heavy involvement in the arrangement of the Fitzroy-Howard marriage. Contemporary evidence suggests that Anne Boleyn was the driving force behind the match, sources from the bride's mother, the Duchess of Norfolk stating that 'Queen Anne got the marriage clear for my lord my husband.' Historians Nikki Clarke and Mathew Lyons conclude that the reason for Anne's involvement being that Henry Fitzroy's potential to marry a princess or noble lady from another land could have caused a threat to Anne, given that King Henry VIII had attempted to negotiate such marriages for his illegitimate son prior to Anne's ascendancy.

I tried to stay true to their 'testy' relationship in The Hopeful Duke in order to shed light on this lesser-known part of the Tudor era, Fitzroy often being a forgotten character in the popular time period, but one which I believe to have struggled with his place in the world.

Henry VIII's continuous back and forth as to his dedication to his son must have been difficult for the boy, made worse still by Queen Katherine of Aragon's resentment of him as well as Anne Boleyn's view of him as a threat to her and her children's futures.

- Henry Fitzroy's titles including Henry VIII's intention of creating him King of Ireland are also true.
- King Henry VIII's <u>warning</u> to his son of Anne's intentions to poison him and Princess Mary is also true, though whether she actually did plot to do so has no evidence to support it.
- Henry Fitzroy's attendance at Anne Boleyn's trial and execution is also factual, for as the king's son, his presence represented the monarch's approval of the event.
- The Second Succession Act of 1536, where Henry VIII had been made able to name any of his children as his heir regardless of their legitimacy, is also factual, and many believed that he would have named Henry Fitzroy in the event that Jane Seymour did not produce a son. This act was passed just days before Fitzroy's death as depicted in The Hopeful Duke.

If you enjoyed The Hopeful Duke please remember to leave a kind review on Amazon or Goodreads, or tell your friends about it!

Printed in Great Britain
by Amazon